Charlie's Promise

Annemarie Allan

pokey
hat

First published in 2017 by Pokey Hat

Pokey Hat is an imprint of Cranachan Publishing Limited

Copyright © Annemarie Allan 2017

ISBN: 978-1-911279-15-0

eISBN: 978-1-911279-16-7

Cover photographs

© shutterstock.com / Tamara Kulikova

© Can Stock Photo Inc. / Paha_L

Cover Design and Typesetting by Cranachan

www.cranachanpublishing.co.uk

@cranachanbooks

For my father

Contents

Free Port of Danzig, November 1938

Jozef tugged his mother's coat from its hook. He wrapped it round his body and crouched down with his back against the wall, wrinkling his nose at the mingled odours of cabbage and coal dust, coats and old shoes. It was as if all the residents of this rickety old building, past and present, had left some trace of themselves in the dark little cupboard.

From outside came the muffled whump of an explosion, followed by the tinkle of breaking glass. Shouts and wild laughter echoed up and down the street. Jozef pulled his mother's coat tightly round his shoulders, remembering the tremor in her voice and her shaking hands when she pushed him inside and ordered him to stay there until she opened the door.

He shifted his cramped legs and then froze when the street door below crashed open. Heavy footsteps pounded up the stairs, followed by a thunderous knocking on the door at the end of the hall. Jozef slid slowly upright, his heart hammering in his chest, thinking of his mother, alone out there, in the splintered, broken remnants of their home.

He heard more shouting from outside and then the sound of footsteps running back downstairs. The street door slammed shut and he slumped down, straining his ears to listen. He could hear nothing, no movement on the other side of the cupboard door. Was his mother still there? Or would he emerge to find the rooms dark and deserted, his mother gone, just like his father and so many of the people he once knew?

That fear kept him in place all through the long night of screams and laughter and breaking glass, until at last he fell into a restless doze, his body and his mind numbed by unbearable tension.

Someone called his name and he jerked awake. Rubbing his eyes, he stumbled into the hall. His mother pulled him towards her, squeezing so tightly he could hardly breathe. He squirmed away and she let him go, reaching for their outdoor clothes.

Soon, they were hurrying along empty streets lined with tall, narrow houses, across roads and pavements where broken glass glittered like winter frost. His heavy coat bounced against his knee, a constant reminder of the package his mother had stitched inside the hem.

He opened his mouth to ask where they were going, but the sound of a car in the distance sent her hurrying down an alley. She grabbed his arm hard enough to hurt, but his yelp of protest was cut short by her hand across his mouth. Together, they slipped like ghosts through the darkness, emerging at the other end of the narrow passage to find the broad sweep of the river directly ahead.

Hugging the shadows, his mother rushed him on, past dingy little shops, their windows filled with rope and sailcloth and other things to do with ships and the sea that he could not name. At last she stopped beside a grimy tub of a vessel with steam already pumping from its filthy smokestack.

There was a man at the foot of the gangplank, a pipe clenched between his yellow teeth. After a hurried conversation, a handful of coins passed from his mother's hand into the sailor's grimy paw. The man grinned, rubbing his thumb and finger together in a universal gesture. She shook her head. The two adults stared at each other for a long moment until finally she pushed Jozef forward. He didn't want to let her go. She had to peel his fingers from her arm one by one.

'*Libn`du, Jozef.*'

He looked up at her in surprise as she wrapped her arms around him and hugged him hard. There was the briefest sensation of a kiss on the top of his head before he was hustled up the narrow wooden plank on to the ship, leaving his mother standing on the quayside. Only then did he understand. He struggled to free himself, fighting against the rough hands that held him. But it was too late.

Chapter 1

Warships in the Mist

'The dog, Charlie! Catch the dog!'

Laddie came barrelling towards Charlie, panicked beyond sense by the meat tin wedged on the end of his pointed nose. Charlie knew he didn't stand a chance. The dog crashed into him with a thump that knocked all the breath from his body and he toppled backwards, landing flat on his back in a muddy puddle.

'Why didn't you stop him?'

Charlie looked up at Jean in disbelief. 'You must be joking!'

But she was already turning away, her anxious eyes following the black and white shape as the wild-eyed dog hurtled across the washing green, his tail between his legs and his paws pounding the ground. Whooping with excitement, a crowd of boys abandoned their football game and set off in pursuit.

'Leave him alone! You're frightening him!'

The dog disappeared down the cobbled lane that led out of the Haven and on to the shore road. Jean took off after him, her blonde pigtails flying, leaving Charlie to clamber awkwardly to his feet. He bent to pick up the book Laddie had knocked out of his hands. The cover was bent, its pages streaked with dirt. He heard footsteps on the stone stairway behind him, then his mother's voice, shrill with annoyance.

'That dog's nothing but a thief.'

His mother wasn't keen on dogs, especially not strays like Laddie. Most of the grown-ups put up with Laddie because he was popular with the children, but there were limits. A thieving dog wasn't welcome in the homes of Morison's Haven.

'It was only an empty can!'

'And would you look at what he's done to the book your grandad gave you! You're nearly twelve years old, Charlie. I expected you to take better care of it than this.'

She reached out and snatched the book from his hands, smoothing the pages so hard he was afraid it might fall to pieces. Charlie opened his mouth to point out that it wasn't really Laddie's fault, but then he closed it again. There was no point in arguing with his mother. It was easier to stay out of the way until she calmed down.

'I'm off to the harbour,' he said. 'Grandad told me there's a boat leaving on the next tide.'

'Good.' She turned away, still clutching the book. 'You could do with the exercise.'

The harbour was one of his grandfather's favourite places, though he had never been a sailor. His working life had been spent deep underground, a miner in the pit along the road. After all those years in the dark, Charlie thought he understood why the old man spent so much time outdoors in all kinds of weather.

Charlie set off for the shore road, grateful that his mother hadn't noticed the mess he'd made of his jacket. There was no sign of anyone else. The rest of the children had been moving too fast for him to catch up, even if he had wanted to. He crossed the road and made his way slowly down the slippery grass slope, moving slowly and awkwardly.

His grandfather was leaning on the harbour wall. He welcomed Charlie with a smile. 'How's Treasure Island?'

'Wet,' said Charlie. 'Sorry, Grandad.'

'Wasn't your fault, son,' his grandfather said when he heard the story. 'Let's just hope the book survives the soaking—and yer mother's cleaning.'

Charlie nodded. They stood for a while in silence, watching the sailors moving about on the boat that was waiting for the tide.

A man emerged from the low doorway of the harbourmaster's house and stumped his way towards them, smoke rising from the pipe gripped between his teeth.

'That'll be the captain.' His grandfather waited until the man drew closer, then he nodded a greeting. 'Tide's up,' he said. 'Ye'll soon be on yer way.'

The captain took the pipe from his mouth. He studied the old man and the boy, his eyes lingering a little too long on Charlie's foot. 'Last boat. There will be no more, I think.'

'Well, I wish ye luck on yer voyage.'

'And I wish you luck with my cargo.' The man gave them a hard-edged smile without any warmth or humour, then he set off for his boat, once more puffing furiously on his pipe.

'He's lucky the tide is high at this time of year,' said his grandfather. 'The harbour hasn't been dredged for a long time. And coal is a heavy load.'

'Why did he come here, then?' asked Charlie. 'Why didn't he go to Leith?'

His grandfather shrugged. 'More profit, I suppose. Coal's cheaper straight out of the pit. Better quality, too.'

'Look Grandad.' Charlie pointed at a sailor who appeared on deck as the captain approached the boat.

'He's carrying a gun!'

'So he is.'

The old man eyed the rifle cradled in the sailor's arms. He put one hand on Charlie's shoulder.

'They won't shoot us, Grandad.'

But his grandfather kept his hand where it was until the stubby little boat had eased its way out of the harbour, threading a complicated route between the rocks that lurked below the surface. Far out on the water, a huge grey ship was moving down the river towards the sea. Even from this distance, the gun turrets rising above the main deck were clearly visible.

'I was a soldier once.'

Charlie looked up with interest. His grandfather hardly ever talked about the war.

'The war to end all wars, they called it. We thought there would never be another.' There was a bitter edge to the old man's voice as he watched the great bulk of the warship heading downriver. 'And now we've got gunships back in the Firth of Forth.'

'Ma said you enlisted,' said Charlie. 'You didn't have to go.'

'That's right.' His grandfather cleared his throat. 'The country wanted us down the pit, but it's a hard life being a miner—back breaking work, sometimes up to yer knees in the freezing water that runs down the tunnels. The water pump is like yer own heartbeat. Ye don't notice it until it stops—and then ye'd better get out fast if ye don't want to drown down there in the dark.'

His eyes drifted towards the pit, where the wheel of the winding gear was outlined against the dreich November sky.

'I thought I was going on a grand adventure,' he went on, 'but I was a fool, Charlie. It was nothing but mud and barbed wire and dead bodies piled up all around—people who had been yer friends. And the bombs exploding day and night, until ye thought the noise would drive ye mad.'

His eyes dropped to the heavy boot on Charlie's twisted foot. Charlie knew he was thinking that his grandson, at least, would never be a soldier. He pulled away, dislodging the hand from his shoulder. His grandfather sighed.

'Believe me, Charlie, there's nothing glorious about war.'

'They made us practise wearing gas masks at school last week,' said Charlie. 'It was horrible—like putting your head in a smelly sack. One of the wee ones was sick.'

'Gas masks. For bairns.' His grandfather's eyes took on a distant look as though his mind was somewhere far in the past, then he plastered a smile on his face and began to rummage around in his pockets.

The old man didn't want to talk about the war any more —and Charlie wasn't sure he wanted to talk about it either. He had the uncomfortable feeling he might hear things he'd rather not know.

'This is for you.' His grandfather held out a coin.

'Thanks, Grandad,' said Charlie. He sighed. 'Ma's saving for my uniform for the grammar school.'

The old man dug in his pocket once more. 'Then ye'd better have another one for yourself.'

Charlie grinned at him, even though he knew his mother wouldn't let him keep the extra penny. 'She's already bought the tie and I haven't even passed the exam yet!'

'You will, Charlie,' said his grandfather. He shook his head in wonderment. 'Twelve years old next month. It seems no time at all since ye were born.'

His grandfather turned away from the harbour and began plodding up the hill. Charlie followed along behind until they reached the top, where the old man stopped at the sight of a solitary figure standing on the other side of the road. She was chewing on a pigtail, peering into the woods on the other side of the gap in the tumbledown wall.

'Is that Jean Baird?'

Charlie nodded.

'Ah hope she's not thinking of going into the woods. It's not safe. Ye'd better go and fetch her.'

His grandfather waved goodbye and left him to it. He clearly didn't know Jean Baird very well. No-one could make Jean do something she didn't want to do. All the same, Charlie crossed the road, prepared to do his best.

'Charlie!' Jean took the braid from her mouth. 'You've got to help me. Jimmy Doig tried to grab hold of Laddie, but he was too rough. Laddie jumped the wall and ran into the woods. He's still in there somewhere!'

Across the wall the trees crowded thickly together, forming an almost impenetrable barrier. Ropes of ivy, some as thick as Charlie's arm, stretched up among the naked branches to form a dense green ceiling that cut out most of the light.

'Nobody's allowed in there,' he said. 'It's dangerous.'

His grandfather had told him about the old mine shaft deep in the wood. It was overgrown now, lost among the trees, abandoned since the day the earth collapsed, leaving two men dead beneath a ton of rubble. Charlie shivered. As far as he knew the bodies—or what was left of them—were still there.

He turned to look at Jean. 'You know Laddie always comes back when he's hungry.'

She raised her eyebrows. 'And exactly how is the dog going to do that if he can't see where he's going?'

Jean had a point. By now Laddie was probably hysterical with terror. And Charlie could all too easily imagine what people would say if he walked away now and left her to go into the woods on her own.

'We'll have a quick look,' he said. 'But we're not going far.'

'Thanks Charlie.' Jean smiled in relief. She glanced down at his feet. 'I'd better go first. The ground is probably pretty bumpy in there.'

He shot her an angry look as he brushed past her and clambered awkwardly over the break in the wall, heading for the darkness beneath the trees.

CHAPTER 2

Into the Woods

The stillness was broken only by the creak of winter-bare branches rubbing against each other. Charlie heard a rustle in the ivy and looked up to see a hooded crow, its head tilted to one side, staring down at him as though questioning his decision to step inside the wood.

'You and me both,' Charlie muttered as he moved forward. He could see no flattened grass or broken twigs. There was nothing that might help him work out where the dog had gone.

'Wait Charlie! I'm stuck!'

Jean was struggling to free herself from a bramble bush that had sunk its barbs into her skirt. Charlie took one more look around then he plodded back towards her.

'Are you sure Laddie came this way?'

'I saw him jump the wall and he didn't come out again. He must be in here somewhere.' Jean unhooked the last of the thorns and moved towards him. 'It's a bit creepy in here, isn't it?'

Charlie nodded, hoping she had changed her mind about searching the wood, but she only waited expectantly until he moved on, picking his way carefully across tumbled piles of fallen branches and loose rock. His balance was never good on uneven surfaces like this. Jean followed close behind, stopping every now and then to unhook her skirt from the thorns that lurked everywhere.

'Watch out, Charlie,' she snapped, when he let go of a branch and it slapped her in the face.

'I'm doing my best,' Charlie snapped back.

He was finding it hard to hard to keep his imagination under control in the dark and silent wood. He couldn't stop thinking about his hero, Jim Hawkins, when he was hiding from the pirates who turned the wooded slopes of Treasure Island into a battleground. There were no bloodthirsty pirates lurking in here, he told himself firmly. Just one boy, one girl, and one lost dog.

He trudged on, fighting his way through the undergrowth, struggling to avoid low-lying branches and the brambles that scratched his bare legs beneath his grey school shorts. Finally he decided they had gone far enough.

'This is no good,' he stopped and turned to face Jean.

'We don't even know that Laddie came this way. He could be anywhere.'

'You've probably been leading us round in circles,' she said. 'Maybe you should give me a turn at the front.'

'Fine,' he said, through gritted teeth. 'Be my guest. I'm sure you can do a lot better than me.'

'Thanks Charlie.' Jean grinned at him, cheerfully ignoring his sarcasm. 'And thanks for coming with me.'

'Only a little bit further,' he said. 'And then I'm going back. With or without you.'

It was an empty threat and Jean knew it as well as he did. The trouble he would be in if he had left her to enter the wood on her own was nothing compared to what people would say if he abandoned her now.

Struggling to ignore the ache in his twisted foot, Charlie forced himself on, unwilling to admit, even to himself, that he no longer had any idea of where they were or how to find their way back.

At last, with a sudden surge of relief, he realised he could see daylight ahead. They must have walked all the way through the wood. Once they got out from under the trees, it would be easy to follow the edge of the wood until they got to the Haven. Laddie would just have to take his chances—assuming he wasn't already safe and sound back home.

Half-blinded by twigs and branches, they hurried towards the patch of brightness, Charlie's mood lightening with every step, until he took a different route to the one Jean was following and felt a stab of horror when he realised his outstretched foot was resting on nothing but empty air.

He found himself staring down at a huge hole in the earth. With a jerk that wrenched his whole body, he threw himself backwards, landing with a thump that jarred him from head to toe. He struggled to his feet, taking one backward step after another away, his legs trembling in anticipation of the ground giving way beneath him and sending him tumbling on to the rocks below.

He stopped at what he hoped was a safe distance from the hole. It was wider than the school playground and horribly deep. Among the heaps of tumbled boulders, a pile of rotting timbers was all that remained of the collapsed mine. With a shiver of dread he remembered his grandfather telling him how the survivors attacked the rocks with picks and shovels and even their bare hands until they finally accepted that there was no hope of reaching the men trapped beneath the piles of rock.

Jean peered over his shoulder. 'What's that?'

'I think it's the old pit.' Charlie said no more. He was positive she wouldn't want to know.

She slid round to stand beside him. 'Maybe we can climb down there and back up the other side.'

'Don't be daft.' Charlie pointed to the massive slabs of rock that littered the ground. 'Even if we got down in one piece, we'd never get across. We have to turn back.'

'What about over there? We could cross that. It looks pretty solid. And it's wide enough.'

With a sinking sensation in his stomach, Charlie saw that Jean was eyeing a thick outcrop of rock that curved around one side of the pit.

'No,' he said. 'We have to go back.'

But then the silence was shattered by a mournful howl. Charlie groaned. The dog had chosen the worst possible moment to reveal his presence.

'It's Laddie!' Jean's eyes lit up. 'He's over there—on the other side!'

Charlie chewed his lip, wishing now that he had never agreed to step inside the wood.

'You don't have to come with me.' Jean's voice broke the silence.

There was a red mark on her cheek where the branch had hit her and scratches on her arms and legs, but he knew Jean wasn't going to give up. And he knew he couldn't let her do it on her own.

Jean took a deep breath, grabbed hold of a sturdy branch and stepped on to the rock. She twisted round to face Charlie.

'It's all right,' she said. 'It's solid.'

Charlie followed, shifting his grip from tree to tree as they inched their way around the edge of the pit. They were only a few steps from the other side when a piece of rock crumbled beneath Charlie's feet and he lost his balance. He yelled out in panic as he slid sideways, tightening his arms around the branch he was holding on to, praying it was sturdy enough to hold his weight.

Jean turned to look at him, her eyes wide with fear. He glared at her.

'I told you this was a stupid idea!'

She was scared too, he could tell. She stood where she was while Charlie kept his arms locked tight around the branch. He didn't want to let it go, but he had no choice. He couldn't stay there forever and it would take even longer to go back than to go forward.

'Charlie,' Jean said in a small voice. 'We have to...'

'*I know*,' he hissed. 'Give me a second to catch my breath.'

Jean nodded, waiting for him to loosen his hold on the branch.

'All right,' he said at last. 'Let's go!'

One behind the other they scurried forward on to solid ground. Jean let loose a high-pitched, shaky laugh.

'We did it!'

They exchanged a quick smile of triumph and then pushed their way through the bushes to find themselves at the top of a shallow dip filled with a drift of soggy leaves. The mud around the edge was scarred with fresh claw marks, but that wasn't the only proof the dog had been here. Somehow, Laddie had managed to get rid of the tin. And somebody else had picked it up.

CHAPTER 3

A Mysterious Stranger

The boy in the hollow looked up at them wild-eyed, like a startled deer, his bright blue eyes the only spot of colour in his pale, mud-streaked face. Jean turned to Charlie with a puzzled frown.

'Who on earth is *that*?'

Apart from visitors to the harbour, strangers were rare in Morison's Haven—and with his filthy coat and matted, dirt-stiffened hair, this boy was stranger than most.

Charlie shrugged. 'I've never seen him before.'

He kept his voice low, knowing that the boy was ready to run. But then the boy's shoulders sagged. He looked down at the tin in his hands and sank down on the pile of soggy leaves with his head bowed, looking small and defeated.

Jean set off down the slope towards him with Charlie following behind, his arms flailing as he struggled to keep his balance. He arrived at the bottom in an undignified slither but luckily Jean didn't notice. She was chewing the end of her pigtail again while she studied the boy, clearly wondering what to do next.

The boy held out the tin and began to speak, his voice swift and urgent. Jean frowned and sent a questioning glance in Charlie's direction, but he could make no sense of the sounds he heard coming from the boy. He couldn't even tell where one word ended and another began.

'He wants to give us the tin,' said Jean. 'He must think that's what we've come for.'

The boy's eyes darted from Jean to Charlie and back again. It reminded Charlie of the way he watched the doctors on his annual visit to the hospital, stretched out on a hard leather couch in nothing but his underwear while he struggled to make sense of the incomprehensible conversation going on around him.

'It's all right,' Jean leaned forward, making sure to keep her voice low. 'You can keep the tin. We don't want it.'

Her gentle tone seemed to reassure the frightened stranger. Slowly, the tension drained from his body. He dropped the tin and began making a pointless effort to brush some of the muck off his clothes.

Charlie took a small step forward and tapped his chest. 'My name's Charlie,' he said, trying to speak slowly

22

and clearly. 'What...'

But he was interrupted by a sudden noise. All three turned to see Laddie erupt from the bushes, barking wildly as he galloped down the hill towards them.

The boy leaped to his feet and raced across the hollow, clawing his way up the opposite side in a frantic tangle of arms and legs. Seconds later, he was gone.

Laddie jumped up and licked Jean's face, still barking enthusiastically.

'Get *down* Laddie!' She pushed him away and turned to Charlie.

'Do you think he's one of the travelling folk?'

Charlie shook his head. 'No. They've been gone for ages.'

The travellers followed the harvest, moving from place to place, living in tents and caravans. They had left the area over a month ago when the last of the potatoes had been dug up and taken to market. The boy couldn't possibly have been here that long.

'Did you hear the way he spoke?' Charlie asked as he followed Jean across the hollow.

'It sounded like nonsense to me.'

'I'm not so sure,' said Charlie. 'It was a bit like the way the sailors talk.'

'You think he's off that boat? The one that left this

23

morning?' Jean stopped, a worried frown creasing her forehead. 'We need to tell someone.'

But Charlie wasn't so sure. 'It doesn't look as if he wants to be found, does it? Not if he's hiding in here. Maybe he was a stowaway.'

Jean laughed. 'You read too many books. Your imagination is running wild, Charlie MacNair!'

Charlie scowled. Jean hadn't been down at the harbour. She hadn't seen that grim-faced sailor with the gun cradled in his arms. And maybe she hadn't looked closely enough at the boy to see the bruises beneath the dirt. If he had come off that boat, it didn't seem likely that he would want to go back. In any case, it was too late. The boat was gone.

Jean took hold of the scruff of Laddie's neck in case he was thinking of running off again and began to pull the dog along with her. 'I have to get back,' she said. 'I'm supposed to be hanging up the washing.'

At the top of the hollow, Charlie paused and glanced behind him. There was nothing to see, apart from the empty tin lying among the leaves. He could almost believe the whole episode had been nothing more than a dream.

He caught up with Jean at the edge of the old mine shaft. She was staring doubtfully at the slab of rock where Charlie had almost toppled into the pit.

'I'm not sure I can get back over. Not if I have to keep hold of Laddie too.'

Charlie wasn't keen on the crossing either, even though he didn't have the dog to worry about.

'Maybe we can go that way.' He pointed to a faint track leading away from the pit, then he picked up a fallen branch and gave the tangled brambles a hearty whack. 'We can beat a path with this.'

'Good idea!' Jean found a stick for herself and together they forced their way through the undergrowth, walloping at the thorny branches that barred their way. Laddie trailed along behind them. A few minutes later, they emerged from the trees to find themselves only a short distance from the gap in the wall.

'I thought it would take us a lot longer than that,' said Jean. 'We must have gone an awfully roundabout route. I suppose it's hard to walk in a straight line when you can't see anything except trees.'

Charlie nodded, grateful that she didn't seem inclined to blame him for leading them astray. And at least it had been easy to find their way back out again. They had left a trail of flattened weeds all the way to the hollow, but it wasn't likely that anyone would notice. Nobody ever came in here. Except for that filthy, starving boy. He needed help, that much was obvious. Charlie wished they could have persuaded him to come with them to the Haven, but he knew that was impossible. The boy had been too frightened.

Jean was thinking about something else. 'Doesn't your grandad give you pocket money on Saturday mornings?'

'I don't get to keep it,' said Charlie. 'Ma always takes it off me.'

'Your Ma doesn't need it as much as he does,' she said. 'I don't know where that boy came from, but I do know that he's lost and he's hungry. We can't leave him there.'

'I don't think he'll want to come anywhere near us again. He was too scared of the dog.'

'Oh, he'll come all right, Charlie,' answered Jean with total confidence. 'If there's something to eat, he'll come.'

He didn't want to admit it, but Jean was right. It was the only way to get the boy to understand that they were friends, not enemies.

She sighed. 'There's no way Ma will let me out of her sight again today. We might have to wait until tomorrow.'

The very thought made Charlie deeply uncomfortable. He put his hand in his pocket and closed his fist around the coins his grandfather had given him. He could at least make sure the boy had food, even if he was still sleeping rough in the woods on a cold November night.

'I'll get him something to eat,' he said. 'I'll come back this afternoon.'

'Great!' Jean looked at him with shining eyes, before she spoilt things by adding, 'are you sure you can do it all by yourself?'

CHAPTER 4

Hide and Seek

'Hey Charlie! What have you got there?'

Charlie's heart sank. It was Jimmy Doig. Jimmy's idea of sharing food was to let you keep the bag while he took care of the contents. If Jimmy got his hands on the broken biscuits, there would very soon be nothing left.

Charlie glanced around. On the other side of the road was the sea wall, with the waves lapping against the rocks below. On this side was the pit, with its sprawling collection of machinery and buildings. It was separated from the road by nothing more than a low wall, but every child in the Haven knew that crossing the wall was absolutely forbidden.

He watched Jimmy walk slowly towards him, knowing that he couldn't move fast enough to get away. In any case, with the pit on one side and the sea on the other, there was nowhere to hide. Charlie wondered if he should say that the biscuits were for his mother, but Jimmy would probably escort him all the way home to make sure he was telling the truth. It was all too easy to imagine the look on his mother's face when he turned up with a bag of broken biscuits instead of the money she was expecting.

It was the pit or the sea. There was no other choice. Taking a deep breath, Charlie stepped over the wall and hurried round the side of the shed where the surface workers sorted the coal and loaded it into the waiting trucks. The clanking rattle of the conveyor belt told him there was no point in trying to hide in there. If the belt was working, the shed would be full of people.

He crouched down in the shadows. The engine house was only a short distance away, but its heavy wooden doors were almost certainly locked.

Jimmy appeared and Charlie shrank back even further. Jimmy smiled. He took a step towards Charlie, but then the sound of heavy footsteps sent him scurrying back around the corner. Charlie hunched even closer into the wall as a man strode past. He was heading for the engine house and Charlie could hardly believe his luck when he saw him climb the steps, pull open the door and walk inside without closing the door behind him. Charlie grinned. It was too good an opportunity to miss.

He pushed the biscuits into his jacket pocket and rose

to his feet, brushing black dust and gritty cinders from his bare knees, then he scuttled across the open space to the engine house. He was up the steps and through the door as fast as he could manage.

He felt a trembling in the metal stair beside him and looked up to see a pair of heavy boots disappearing upwards. Head tilted, he stood where he was, mesmerised by the sight of the massive piston moving back and forth, then he dragged his eyes away and glanced around. There was a huge iron cylinder fixed to the floor with bolts as big as the palm of his hand.

Charlie crossed the floor and slid down into the space between the cylinder and the wall. All he had to do now was to keep an eye out for the man coming back down and sneak out of the door in front of him. By then, with a bit of luck, Jimmy would have given up and gone away.

The noise from the beam engine was hypnotic. Like his grandfather and everyone else in the Haven, Charlie had lived with the beat of the engine all his life. It was so much a part of the background that he hardly heard it any more. In here, though, the noise battered at his ears and shook his body till he was dizzy. He tried to focus on the gaps in the metal staircase, watching for any sign of movement, but the endless to and fro of the machinery made it almost impossible to concentrate.

As he raised his hands to cover his ears, he felt a movement in the air behind him. A fist closed around his shirt collar and he was lifted into the air. Half choked, he wriggled and twisted, struggling to catch his breath. When his captor turned him round, Charlie found himself looking into a face that was crimson with rage. He understood now why the door hadn't been locked. Someone else had already been inside.

The man's lips were moving. The noise from the engine drowned his words but Charlie didn't need to hear what he was saying to know that he was absolutely furious. He shook Charlie like a dog and hauled him towards the door. A heavy boot connected with Charlie's backside and he tumbled down the steps, landing with a thud that snapped his teeth together.

'Get out of here!' The voice came dimly through the ringing in his ears. 'And don't come back. This is no place for daft bairns and their stupid games!'

The door slammed shut, leaving Charlie sitting in the dirt. Slowly, the world returned to normal, bringing with it the sound of the cage clanking its way up from the underground workings of the mine. A babble of voices told him that the cage was almost at the surface. He knew he had to get moving. If anyone told his father or his brother Martin that he had been seen hanging around the pit, he would be in serious trouble.

He stood up and limped into the shelter of an overhead walkway, his eyes darting all around in case Jimmy reappeared. If the morning shift down the pit was over, then he would have to hurry if he wanted to be in and out of the woods before dark.

In a series of cautious stops and starts, he crept past the racket from the coal shed and on past the kilns where they made bricks out of the clay that came up from the pit along with the coal. The warm air that hit him as he passed the kilns was so dry he could hardly breathe.

When he finally emerged on to the shore road, he took a careful look up and down to make sure it was deserted before he set off once more on his interrupted journey. Although the houses of the Haven kept their backs to the sea, there were plenty of windows overlooking the road and he felt the hair on the back of his neck prickle uncomfortably as he walked past. Luckily, nobody seemed to be interested in what Charlie MacNair was up to.

It was well into the afternoon by the time he sank down on to the broken wall, his aching backside an uncomfortable reminder of his encounter with the man at the engine house. The day was not yet over but it already felt as though it had lasted for a hundred years.

CHAPTER 5

I Am Jozef

Staggering slightly, Charlie hauled himself to his feet and clambered over the wall. All that walking had strained his bad foot and now his whole leg ached. It was a surprise to discover that the woods, so vast and threatening when he and Jean had been stumbling about, felt far less dangerous now that he knew where he was going and there was a clear path to follow.

In a few minutes, he was at the hollow. He hunted around until he found a flat rock and pulled it into the middle of the dip, then he pulled out the crumpled paper bag and emptied the biscuits on to the rock, where they were clearly visible. With a weary sigh, he sat back, shivering slightly in the damp air. All that effort, for nothing more than a handful of broken biscuits.

The afternoon light began to fade. The wood might feel smaller now than it did this morning, but he still didn't like the idea of sitting in the dark with only the ghosts of those long-dead miners for company. A breeze shook the treetops, sending a solitary sycamore seed twirling through the air. The sound of the branches rubbing together made him think of skeletons on the move. The ground felt cold and damp beneath him and he shifted uneasily, aware that he was getting uncomfortably close to scaring himself silly. Jean was right. He had too much imagination for his own good.

'This is stupid,' he growled to himself, but somehow that didn't seem to help.

A rustle in the bushes caught his attention. He held his breath, watching as the leaves drew apart to reveal a small, anxious face. Charlie forced what he hoped was a friendly smile on to his own face and pointed at the rock. The boy stood up. He took a few steps down the slope then he stopped, his eyes flicking from the rock to Charlie and back again. His body was poised, ready to run at the first hint of danger.

Concentrating on keeping his movements as slow and unthreatening as possible, Charlie leaned forward, lifted one of the biscuits and held it out. The bright blue eyes remained fixed on Charlie's face. No-one had ever looked at him with such suspicion before.

In the end, hunger triumphed over caution. The boy covered the last few yards in a rush and crouched down. He took the biscuit from Charlie's hand and stuffed it into his mouth, his other hand already reaching for more. The biscuits were gone in seconds.

Charlie lifted his hand again. The boy flinched, but he stayed where he was. Charlie pointed to himself.

'Charlie,' he said, slowly and clearly. 'My name is Charlie.' Then he pointed at the boy and raised his eyebrows to make the question clear.

The boy chewed furiously until the last morsel was gone, then he reached down and cleared a space among the leaves. Charlie craned forward to watch as the boy traced some letters in the dirt.

'Jozef,' he read aloud, wondering why the boy had chosen to write instead of speak. Perhaps he thought that he wouldn't be understood, or maybe he wanted to show Charlie that he was more than some wild creature of the woods.

The boy smiled and nodded and tapped his chest. 'Jozef!'

Charlie felt something shift inside his head as he matched Jozef's smile with a smile of his own, a connection that hadn't been there before. With a name, Jozef somehow became more of a person and for some reason that made the state he was in even worse. His torn, filthy coat hung loose on his skinny body and his hair was so stiff with dirt that Charlie couldn't even guess at its colour, but it was obvious he hadn't always been like this. The coat was good quality cloth and his scuffed shoes were city shoes, nothing like the sturdy boots worn by children from the Haven.

Charlie made up his mind. He couldn't leave Jozef here. His mother would probably be horrified when he turned up with this ragged foreigner, but at least she would feed him and keep him warm until she decided what to do with him.

Very slowly, Charlie stood up. He pointed to the path he and Jean had trodden through the grass and then held out his hand. Jozef's eyes clouded with doubt and suspicion. He jumped up, then turned and ran for the bushes, leaving Charlie alone in the hollow, staring glumly at the scatter of crumbs left on the stone. There was nothing for it but to go home.

Back at the Haven, he wanted nothing more than to drag himself upstairs into his house, but Jean was waiting for him at the foot of the steps. Her little sister Maggie was close by, swinging round and round the washing pole. He nodded in answer to Jean's enquiring look, but he didn't stop to talk. Instead, he slid past her and up the steps to his own front door.

'So ye finally decided to come home?' His mother's voice came from the scullery, where she was washing dishes. 'Thomas ate yer tea. There's bread and dripping. And ye can count yourself lucky to have that!'

Charlie made for the table and grabbed a slice of bread, grateful to get off so lightly. Nobody worried much about what the children got up to during the day, but missing a meal was a major crime.

'Where's yer penny?'

The bread dropped from his hand. He hadn't expected her to ask for it so soon. When he turned round, she was standing behind him, drying her hands on her apron.

'I lost it.'

Her chin came up and her eyes narrowed. 'Lost it?'

She looked him up and down, taking in his muddy coat and his mucky knees. A frown creased her forehead.

He knew what she was thinking. 'Nobody took it off me, Ma.'

The frown deepened and with a sudden burst of inspiration he added, 'I really did lose it. That's why I'm late. I was trying to find it.'

He felt a stab of guilt when he saw her face soften slightly. He didn't usually lie to his mother.

'Well,' she said. 'I suppose we'll have to do without. But

be more careful next time. Money doesn't grow on trees.'

Sagging in relief, Charlie turned back to the table. He sat down and ate quickly, too tired even to taste what he crammed into his mouth. When he was finished, he made straight for the back bedroom. It wasn't all that late, but it had been a very long day.

He unlaced his boots and dropped them on the floor, dumping his clothes in a pile beside them before he climbed thankfully into bed. His brother Thomas worked the night shift along with Charlie's father so Charlie had the bed to himself until the early hours of the morning, when Thomas finished his shift.

His book was on the chair beside the bed, its pages crinkled but still intact. He reached out for it and began to read, but for once he couldn't manage to lose himself in the story of Jim Hawkins and the search for Treasure Island. Eventually, he gave up, tucked the book under his pillow and stretched out, warm and comfortable, trying not to think about the boy in the woods who was still outside in the dark, cold and hungry and all alone.

'Jozef,' he reminded himself. 'His name is Jozef.'

Charlie drifted off to sleep. Outside, the children called to each other as they gathered beneath the single street lamp. None of them saw the shadow that crept towards the houses. It crouched, invisible, watching them as they slipped in and out of the pool of light, their shouts and laughter echoing off the surrounding walls. The shadow sat there for a long time before it finally drifted away into the darkness.

Chapter 6

Sign Language

His mother raised an eyebrow when she saw Jean waiting at the door the next morning. Boys didn't play with girls— not unless the boy was a total softie. She didn't say anything though. She probably thought that if he was with Jean, then he wouldn't come home in a state like he did yesterday— which went to show how little she really knew.

Charlie stopped at the foot of the stair. 'Where's Maggie?'

Jean almost always had her little sister trailing along behind, but today there was no sign of her.

Jean scowled. 'I made a deal with Mary. She took Maggie to the shore along with her wee brothers. I have to look after them this afternoon.'

But then her face brightened. She reached into the pocket of her skirt and pulled out several slices of bread.

'I managed to get some food for the boy in the wood. It wasn't easy. Ma thought we ate enough for an army this morning. Poor Maggie couldn't understand where half her breakfast went!'

Charlie stuck his hand down his shirt and produced two slices of toast stuck together with jam. He had pleaded last night's missing supper as an excuse for eating more than he usually did.

'I'm not sure we can keep this up,' he said as they made their way along the road. 'Jozef needs more than this.'

Jean smiled. 'So that's his name! Now we've got something to call him instead of 'that boy'.'

'Jean!' The warning note in Charlie's voice wiped the smile off her face. 'He can't stay in the woods. We can't look after him ourselves.'

'We don't have a choice,' she insisted. 'If he came off that boat, he'll be in a lot of trouble if anyone finds him. He's a foreigner—and you can't just walk into another country.' She waved a hand vaguely in the air. 'There's... laws about it. And anyway, he's scared enough already. What do you think would happen if we fetched Johnnie Crawford?'

Johnnie was the local policeman, a huge bear of a man, red-faced and always sweating in his thick uniform. If Johnnie Crawford came looking for him, Jozef would be terrified.

Jean laid a hand on Charlie's arm. 'Let's give it a couple

of days. If we can keep him fed, then maybe he'll trust us enough to come to the Haven.'

'And what are we going to feed him?' Charlie's voice was glum, thinking of his mother's suspicious look at breakfast.

Jean flashed a smile, taking his words for agreement. 'Come on, Charlie. We'll think of something. We can pinch turnips from the field if we have to!'

She stopped at the gap in the wall, glanced around to make sure no-one was watching and hopped across, unaware of the exasperated look Charlie was directing at her back.

Jozef appeared as soon as they reached the hollow. He must have been waiting for them. The bread was gone in no time. He stared into their faces, clearly thinking hard as he chewed on the handful of dried prunes that Jean had pinched from the cupboard when her mother's back was turned.

At last Jozef seemed to make up his mind. He licked his sticky hands, took hold of the hem of his coat and began to pick at the stitching with his fingers. When the gap was wide enough, he reached inside the hole and pulled out a greasy square of folded cardboard.

Jozef looked down at it, his face still and thoughtful, then he held it out.

Charlie took it from him and unfolded it slowly. Jozef watched, his eyes fixed on Charlie's face. There was a piece of paper tucked inside the cardboard. As Charlie began to open it, a couple of coins dropped out. He bent down and picked them out of the dirt, turning them between his fingers. There was a man's head on one side and on the other a bird with outstretched wings. Jozef leaned forward and tapped the coin with a grimy finger, then he pointed to his mouth.

'He's asking us to buy food,' said Charlie.

'I can see that. I'm not daft,' Jean huffed. She took both coins from Charlie and jingled them together. A thoughtful look appeared on her face.

'You are daft if you're thinking of using them,' said Charlie. 'It's not our kind of money. It'll be no use trying to buy food with it here.'

'Money's money,' she said. 'And how else will we get anything for Jozef to eat?'

Jozef took the scrap of paper from Charlie and pointed to the writing on the inside. Jean leaned across for a closer look.

'David Levy,' she read. 'Acheson's Close, Edinburgh. It's an address! We don't have to worry about Johnnie Crawford. We can take Jozef there ourselves.'

Charlie frowned. 'Don't even think it, Jean.'

'Why not? You've been to Edinburgh lots of times.'

'I haven't. I only go once a year.' He didn't bother to add that his experience of the city was limited to a long tram journey, followed by a bus ride from Princes Street to the Sick Children's Hospital. 'It's a big place, Jean. I don't know how we would find our way. And we've no money to get there.'

Jean waved the coins under his nose. 'We can pay the tram fares with these.'

Charlie was really alarmed now. 'Jean, if you spend that money, we'll get into serious trouble!'

Jean handed Jozef the paper and stowed the coins carefully in her skirt pocket. 'You worry too much. It'll all work out. You wait and see.'

Charlie ground his teeth in frustration. There was nothing he could do to force her to give up the coins. Jean studied Jozef thoughtfully.

'I wonder who David Levy is?'

At the sound of the name, Jozef smiled and jumped to his feet, as though he thought they were leaving immediately. His face fell when he saw Charlie shake his head. Even if they did have money for the fares, the trams didn't run on a Sunday. He had no idea how to explain that, so instead he pointed at the sun and tapped an imaginary watch, trying to suggest that it was too late in the day to go anywhere.

Jozef's face clouded with disappointment. He sat back down and stared miserably at the ground. Charlie and Jean exchanged a look, then Jean knelt down in front of Jozef. With signs and gestures, she managed to ask how he came to be in the wood. Jozef nodded. He got to his feet, filled a pretend pipe and began puffing on it furiously as he stamped up and down.

Jean giggled. 'What's that supposed to be?'

'He's off that boat all right,' said Charlie. 'That's the captain.'

He was beginning to understand. Someone had written out that address and hidden it where no-one would find it. They must have put Jozef on that boat thinking it was heading for Leith, the port nearest to Edinburgh. In a port that size, Charlie guessed that it wouldn't be hard to find a sailor willing to accept foreign coins in exchange for taking Jozef to Acheson's Close.

But the captain hadn't gone to Leith. Instead, he had decided to chance his luck at the much smaller harbour of Morison's Haven. Charlie didn't know whether Jozef had slipped away, or whether he had simply been dumped, but it didn't matter either way. Jozef was miles from the city, without a clue about how to get to Edinburgh and find the address on the piece of paper. Charlie wondered why Jozef had been on the boat in the first place. Where had he come from? And why was he all on his own?

Jean wandered off. Charlie examined the piece of cardboard in his hand. He squinted at the curly writing, struggling to make sense of it.

'*Reisepass.*' He read the word aloud, not at all sure how to say it. There was a large red letter 'J' stamped in the top corner and beneath that, more words that he could barely get his tongue around.

'*Freie Stadt Danzig...?*'

Jozef's face froze. He snatched the card from Charlie's hand and threw it on to the ground, then he stamped on it, grinding it beneath his heel. When he looked back at Charlie, his body was once more stiff with tension.

Charlie was afraid to move or speak in case he did the wrong thing. They stood staring at each other until, to Charlie's relief, Jozef slowly lowered himself back to the ground.

When Jean reappeared, she found the boys with their heads bent over a game, moving twigs around a row of holes scooped out of the dirt. From the look of his hands, it was Jozef who had done the digging. Charlie let out a whoop of triumph and grabbed the last of the sticks. Jozef knelt back on his heels, scowling in disappointment, then he shrugged and held up both hands in defeat. Charlie grinned.

'It's time to go,' said Jean. 'We don't want anyone to come looking for us.'

Charlie hadn't yet given up hope that Jozef might be persuaded to come with them. He stood up and once again held out his hand. This time, Jozef didn't try to run away, but he shook his head firmly. Perhaps he did trust them a little, but not enough. Not yet.

With the help of a bit more mime and play-acting, Jean managed to explain that there was school tomorrow and they wouldn't be able to come until it was over. As they left the hollow, she stopped and turned towards the small hunched figure crouched in the bottom of the dip.

'I found his shelter, Charlie,' she said, with a catch in her voice. 'It's awful. Nothing but a couple of sacks draped over some fallen branches.' She glanced up at the sky. 'He's going to get cold and wet if it rains tonight.'

'We need to let someone know where he is,' said Charlie. 'He could get really sick.'

'I know that,' said Jean. 'But if we come back with a stranger—a grown-up—he'll run off. You know he will.' She chewed on her pigtail, thinking hard. 'Maybe he'll be all right here for another day or so.'

Charlie nodded. If they wanted to get him out of the wood, they had to convince Jozef they meant him no harm. But that wasn't the only thing he was worried about. He stared at the back of Jean's head all the way out of the wood, wishing that those coins had ended up in his pocket instead of Jean's.

Chapter 7

Bread and Chocolate

Charlie woke early the next morning. When he turned to look out of the window he saw that dawn was breaking and the pale-blue sky was laced with whiter streaks of cloud. It was warmer than November had any right to be, but even so, the thought of Jozef, damp and hungry in his makeshift shelter, buzzed around inside his head like a troublesome fly.

His brother Thomas coughed and rolled over, taking most of the covers with him. Charlie sat up, swinging both feet down on to the cold linoleum floor. His clothes were no longer where he had left them. His mother must have come in when he was asleep and now they hung neatly on the back of the chair, brushed and clean, all ready for school.

He didn't get a chance to save anything from breakfast. His mother had a nose for trouble and she kept her eye on him. She knew something was up and she was determined to find out what it was. Charlie kept his head down. As soon as she turned away, he slipped out the front door with a hasty goodbye.

He caught sight of Jean a little way ahead of him, pulling Maggie along with her. She probably hadn't been any luckier than him. Jean couldn't get away with raiding her mother's store cupboard two days in a row.

'Jean,' he said quietly when he caught her up, 'I think you should give Jozef's money to me.'

Jean walked on. 'I'm not stupid, Charlie. I know what I'm doing.'

'You don't know,' he insisted, determined to make his point, while Maggie skipped along beside them, her eyes bright with curiosity. 'You're going to get into serious trouble. You can't...'

He broke off as Jean's friend Mary appeared at his shoulder.

'What are you two whispering about?'

'Nothing important,' snapped Jean. 'Except that Charlie MacNair thinks I'm a fool.'

Charlie gave up and dropped back, leaving the girls to walk on together. His gloom deepened when he saw Jimmy Doig hanging about with a bunch of other boys at the school gates. To his surprise, it wasn't him Jimmy was waiting for.

Instead, he stepped out in front of Jean, a grin spreading across his face.

'I hear you've been spending a fair bit of time with that useless lump over there.' Jimmy jerked his head in Charlie's direction.

'What if I have?' Jean glowered at him.

Jimmy turned to a boy in Charlie's class. 'You saw them coming out of the woods didn't you Donald? Holding hands.'

Donald Ritchie looked puzzled. 'I didn't say they were holding hands.'

Jimmy ignored that. He turned back to Jean, his smile widening even further. 'So... how about a wee trip into the woods with me sometime?'

There was a snort of laughter from the boys. Jean's face went bright red.

'Why would I want to hang around with you? You've got hair like a witch's broom and a face like a bashed tattie.'

Charlie swallowed nervously when he saw the smile on Jimmy's face turn into a ferocious scowl. Jimmy moved closer to Jean, forcing her into the road. Maggie let go of her sister's hand and grabbed Mary's instead. Charlie took a step forward. He wasn't sure what he could do, but he wasn't going to leave Jean to face Jimmy on her own.

But in the end, he didn't have to do anything. The raucous clang of the school bell interrupted them and within seconds, the knot of children at the gate was swept away by latecomers rushing into the playground.

'Saved by the bell!' Jean let loose a nervous giggle as she hurried to join the line of girls.

Charlie sighed. Jean had let her tongue run away with her once too often. It wasn't a good idea to make an enemy of Jimmy Doig.

He waited anxiously all morning for a chance to talk to her. Break time was no good—the girls played in a separate playground. When the bell rang for dinner time, he hurried out of the classroom to see Jean sweep past him in the middle of a crowd of laughing, chattering girls, giving him no opportunity for a quiet word.

His suspicion that she was deliberately avoiding him turned to certainty when school was over and Mary appeared at the gate with Maggie trotting beside her.

'Jean said she had something important to do.' Mary winked at Charlie. 'I thought she was meeting up with you.'

There was no sign of her when he reached the gap in the wall and he arrived at the hollow to find Jozef waiting there alone. It was hard to bear the look of disappointment in his eyes at the sight of the single slice of bread Charlie had managed to save from his midday meal.

A few minutes later, Jean appeared at the top of the dip. Charlie frowned when he saw the grin on her face. She made her way carefully down the slope and placed a fresh loaf of bread and a big slab of chocolate on the ground. Jozef's jaw dropped. Charlie scowled.

'I told you not to touch that money,' he said.

Jean lifted her eyebrows. 'For your information, mister clever, I had no trouble at all. I waited till the shop was really busy. Aggie gave me what I asked for, then she took the money, handed over the change and that was that! You know she can't see anything that isn't right up against her nose.'

Charlie struggled to swallow his anger. Aggie Purdy might be half-blind, but she knew the value of every single penny that passed through her hands. At the very least, she would have noticed that Jean was spending a lot more than usual. But he said nothing. He didn't want to quarrel in front of Jozef.

Twisting off pieces of bread and cramming them into his mouth, Jozef gazed at Jean with shining eyes.

'And that's not all,' Jean said. 'I've thought of a place for Jozef to hide. Someplace nice and dry.'

'Where?' Despite himself, Charlie was interested.

'The brick kilns.' Jean's smile widened.

Jozef's eyes shifted from face to face, frowning in concentration as he tried to grasp what they were talking about.

'Nobody will look in there,' she said. 'They'll be emptying one tomorrow morning and once a kiln's been fired, they leave it to rest for a week.' Jean knew what she was talking about. Her father was a brick maker. 'He'll be safe and warm. And now we've got some money, he won't be hungry anymore.'

Charlie said nothing. There was no point in arguing. It was too late to do anything about it now. Instead, he set his mind to working out the best way to move Jozef without being seen. He was pretty sure Jozef would be willing to come with them tomorrow if they could explain that they had a warm shelter to offer him. It wasn't a permanent solution, but it didn't have to be. You could tell from the way Jozef smiled at Jean that he was learning to trust them. Charlie allowed himself to hope that their problems would soon be over, but Jean's next words made it very clear that her plans did not include passing Jozef over to anyone else.

'There's plenty money left over for the tram fares,' She looked from Charlie to Jozef, clearly delighted with herself. 'We can take him to the address on that piece of paper as soon as school's over for the week.'

Charlie groaned. 'Jean, it's only Monday. There's no way we can keep him hidden that long!'

'Why not?' Jean gave Charlie a superior look. 'We've done a pretty good job so far.'

Jozef stuffed the last of the bread in his mouth and let out an enormous belch. He patted his stomach and grinned. All three of them laughed.

'See you tomorrow, Jozef.' Jean was smiling as they turned away.

Charlie followed, keeping his thoughts to himself. Jean was wrong. Jozef needed more help than they could give him. If she still refused to listen to him, then tomorrow after school he would talk to his brother Thomas—or maybe his grandfather.

He set off for home feeling a bit more cheerful, unaware that tomorrow, when it came, would turn out to be utterly disastrous.

CHAPTER 8

Truth or Consequences

Miss Moncreiff made a neat little tick in the class register and lifted her head.

'Jean Baird? Mr. Munro wants to see you in his office right away.'

From his seat at the back, Charlie saw Jean stiffen. A summons from the headmaster was never good news and Charlie had a horrible feeling he already knew what this one was about.

A few minutes later a small boy shuffled into the classroom. He raised one hand to wipe his runny nose and lowered it hastily when he saw the expression on Miss Moncreiff's face. After a mumbled conversation, Charlie saw her turn in his direction.

'Mr. Munro wants you too, Charlie.'

Charlie's face reddened as the whole class turned to look at him. He stood up and made his way between the rows of desks towards the door, walking as slowly as he could down the corridor. Even so, he reached the headmaster's door far sooner than he would have liked. He gave a tentative knock.

'Enter.'

Charlie took a deep breath, turned the handle and stepped inside.

Mr. Munro stood behind his desk. In silence, he watched Charlie walk towards him. Jean was standing in front of the desk, staring down at the thick leather belt that lay curled on top of the polished wood surface, its end split in two like the tongue of a snake.

'Mrs. Purdy called on me last night,' said the headmaster. 'She said she would rather talk to me than bring trouble on a family by involving the police. I have spoken to Jean and she tells me you know something about this.'

The headmaster looked hard at Charlie from under his heavy eyebrows. He tapped his finger on the coin that lay in front of him.

'Do you know what this is, Charlie?'

Charlie gulped. His legs were shaking so hard his knees were knocking together. 'It's a shilling, sir.'

'Yes, it is,' said Mr. Munro. 'But not from here. This is a German shilling. Jean tells me you gave it to her. She says you got it from your grandfather.'

Charlie felt a brief surge of anger that evaporated almost immediately. Jean must have grabbed at the first thing that came into her head, hoping to explain the existence of the coin without giving Jozef away. He risked a glance in her direction. She had her eyes fixed firmly on the floor. The silence stretched on until he could bear it no longer.

'Yes, sir,' he said at last, his voice quivering.

'I see.' Mr. Munro frowned. 'Perhaps we should send for your grandfather to confirm this?'

'No, sir,' said Charlie quickly. 'He... He doesn't know I took it.'

'Are you telling me you stole it?'

Numbly, Charlie nodded.

'And where, exactly, did your grandfather get this coin?'

'He was in the war, sir,' said Charlie. 'He kept it for a souvenir.'

'Is that so?'

Charlie hadn't thought Mr. Munro could have frowned any harder, but he did. He picked up the coin and held it out, forcing Charlie to take it from him.

'I advise you to look very carefully,' he said. 'Whatever else you might be, I know you are not stupid. The Great War finished in 1918. The date on this coin is 1932.'

Charlie stood with the coin in his sweaty palm while Mr.

Munro reached down and lifted the belt, flexing it between his hands.

'I am very disappointed in you both,' said Mr. Munro. 'Particularly you, Charlie. It seems you are not only a thief, but also a liar.'

From the corner of his eye, Charlie saw that Jean was following the progress of the belt like a hypnotised rabbit. She swayed gently, then gave a small sigh and sank slowly to the floor. Her eyes fluttered briefly and then they closed. Charlie couldn't believe it. Jean had fainted.

'Jean, get up! Jean!'

She was lying on her back on the hard leather bed in the school sick room. Desperate to wake her, Charlie reached out and pinched the skin on the back of her hand.

'Ouch!' Jean's eyes flew open. She snatched her hand away and sat up, her gaze travelling round the green and white walls until they came to rest on Charlie's face.

'What happened?'

'You fainted.'

'I did not.' She glared at him indignantly, then her face fell. She turned her head away from him.

'I made a muck of it, Charlie,' she whispered. 'We'll never be able to help Jozef now. And I got you into trouble as well.'

Charlie knew she was going to be even more upset when she heard what he had to say.

'Mr. Munro thinks there's someone hiding in the woods.'

'Charlie!' She looked at him, horrified.

'I didn't tell! It was Jimmy Doig. Mr. Munro was carrying you to the sick room when Miss Moncreiff came out of the classroom looking for him.'

Jean's face reddened at the thought of the headmaster picking her up like a baby. 'But Jimmy doesn't know about Jozef.'

'Jimmy told Miss Moncreiff that Donald saw both of us in the woods. Mr. Munro put two and two together.'

Charlie shivered, remembering the anger on the headmaster's face when Miss Moncreiff left him to return to her classroom.

'He said we should never have trusted the person who gave us that coin. We should have gone to the police. He's fetching Johnnie Crawford.'

A big fat tear slid down Jean's cheek. 'It's all my fault, isn't it? I made Jimmy angry enough to tell—and I was stupid about the money too.'

Charlie took a deep breath. He couldn't bear the thought of Jozef being hunted through the woods.

'It's not too late,' he said. 'Mr. Munro only left a few

minutes ago. We can get there before they do, but we'll have to be really quick—and really careful.'

He walked to the door, pulled it open and peered outside. They were in so much trouble already, he didn't think it would make much difference if they sneaked out of school.

'There's no-one around,' he said. 'Let's go.'

One behind the other, they scurried down the corridor, out the main entrance and down the steps to the gate. The high classroom windows made it impossible for anyone to see outside—except for Mr. Munro, of course, but he wasn't there.

Jean reached out her hand and Charlie grabbed hold. For once, he was grateful for the help. He couldn't afford to move at his usual slow pace. He held on tightly as she flew down the road, pulling him along in her wake. It wasn't only the speed that left him panting for breath as they scrambled over the wall and rushed along the path towards the hollow. It was the sense of doom that seized hold of him every time he thought of Jozef, patiently waiting, unaware of the disaster unleashed by the coins he had given to Jean.

They broke through the bushes to find Jozef in the hollow. He wasn't alone. Laddie had found himself a new friend, one who didn't disappear for most of the day into the big stone building where dogs were most definitely not welcome.

'Jozef!' Jean yelled. 'You have to get away from here. Right now!'

Jozef's welcoming smile was replaced by a look of surprise, but her words meant nothing to him, not until the bushes parted to reveal Mr. Munro, with Johnnie Crawford close behind.

At the sight of the policeman, Jozef's expression changed from puzzlement to horror and despair.

'Run, Jozef! Run!'

Charlie's desperate instructions were unnecessary. In less than a second, Jozef was up the other side of the hollow and away, while Johnnie Crawford lumbered after him, pushing his way through the bushes, cursing at the dog who danced around his legs, convinced he was taking part in some exciting new game. Jean and Charlie stood there, frozen to the spot by the fury on their headmaster's face.

CHAPTER 9

Decisions

'What did your Ma say?'

It was Wednesday afternoon. School was over for the day and Charlie and Jean were down on the shore where they had found a sheltered space among the rocks, hopefully safe from prying eyes.

Jean made a face. 'She gave me a walloping for bringing the police to the door and told me I was a cheeky besom who'd come to no good in the end. Then she gave me so many jobs to do I didn't have a minute to myself until bedtime. What about you?'

Charlie shrugged. His mother never hit him. It was one of the few benefits of his bad foot, though sometimes he thought he might have preferred a quick thump to one of her cold, disapproving silences.

'Sent to bed without any tea. It was all right though. Thomas sneaked me something to eat before he went to work. After that I read my book until I fell asleep.'

That wasn't quite true. It had been almost impossible to stop thinking about Jozef. For the first time in his life, he found himself wondering what might happen to him if he lost his home and his family. He had never realised before how lucky he was.

'At least they didn't find Jozef,' he said. 'And we didn't get the belt after all.'

They both fell silent, thinking of yesterday's interview with Mr. Munro. To their great surprise and relief, he had reined in his temper, telling them that he understood they had only been trying to help.

'There is no excuse for the fact that you lied to me,' he'd said.

Charlie and Jean had watched him, rigid with tension, waiting for whatever came next.

'However, I have decided to put that to one side for now. If you have any further contact with this boy, I expect you to let me know. Children are not equipped to deal with matters best left to their elders.'

Charlie and Jean had nodded eagerly, grateful to escape without the feel of the heavy leather belt across their hands.

Miss Moncreiff wasn't so forgiving. She had sent a heavy glower in their direction when they arrived in the classroom that morning. It hadn't been easy to make it through the rest of the day without giving her a reason to punish them.

Jean picked up a flat stone and flicked it towards the water with an expert twist of her wrist.

'I'd like to strangle Jimmy,' she said, watching the stone bounce across the still surface of the water. When she spoke again, her voice was barely a whisper. 'I wish I'd never spent that money.'

Charlie couldn't help thinking that she was right, although if he was going to be honest, he had to admit that it was partly his fault for letting her keep the money in the first place. He should have made more of an effort to stop her spending it. All the same, she ought to have known it would make things worse, not better.

He opened his mouth to tell her so, but when she turned towards him he saw the glitter of unshed tears in her eyes. Jean knew as well as he did that she had done something monumentally stupid.

'Well, there's nothing we can do about it now,' he said. 'And at least you got Jozef fed.'

Jean wiped away the tears with an angry gesture. 'Did you see the look on Jozef's face when he saw Johnnie Crawford? He wasn't just afraid, he was absolutely terrified.'

Charlie nodded. 'I think it was the uniform.' He frowned

thoughtfully. 'Maybe it has something to do with the war.'

'No,' said Jean. 'My Dad says there isn't going to be a war. He read it in the paper.'

'But there already is a war,' said Charlie. 'In Europe.'

He didn't care what it said in the newspaper. Those ships on the Firth of Forth, the gas masks handed out at school, the air raid shelter that had been built beneath the old customs house—nobody would make all those preparations without good reason.

'But Jozef's not a soldier,' said Jean. 'He's only a boy. And I don't understand how he ended up here all by himself. What do you think happened to his family?'

Charlie shrugged. He had no answers to offer.

Jean turned her face back to the water. 'I don't suppose it matters any more. I heard Ma saying they searched all through the woods but there was no sign of him. He's probably miles away by now. Even if we did find him, we can't talk to him. We can't explain what happened. He's never going to trust us again.'

Charlie said nothing. He had a ghost of an idea about where Jozef might be, but he didn't want to share it with Jean. Not yet. He needed to check it out for himself. Somehow, whenever he was with Jean, things seemed to spiral out of control.

A small figure appeared on the rocks above them. Jean sighed deeply.

'Ma told Maggie to keep an eye on me. She said she could trust her better than me, even though she's only six.'

Maggie was watching them closely. Her school pinafore had a rip down one side and her face was smeared with muck, but her eyes gleamed with triumph.

'Ma told you to stay away from our Jean, Charlie MacNair!'

Jean sighed again, then she climbed to her feet, brushing the bright flecks of shingle from her skirt.

'I'd better get her home before she does herself any more damage.'

'Jozef will be all right. Honestly, Jean.'

'I hope you're right, Charlie. But at least you don't need to worry about Maggie telling tales. She's always making things up. I'll tell Ma she's lying to get me in trouble.'

Charlie watched her scramble up the rocks and disappear from sight then he turned back to the sea. A small patch of pale afternoon sunlight moved slowly across the shingle. There was only about an hour of daylight left. The tide was coming in fast, bringing with it a clammy bank of fog that local people called the haar. Far out in the distance, ships moved through the haze, huge grey ghosts heading out to sea.

Charlie was sure that the grown-ups were wrong. Jozef wasn't dangerous. He was exactly what he seemed: an innocent refugee from some other world, where men in uniform were enemies to be dreaded and avoided.

He wondered if Mr. Munro was right. Maybe they shouldn't have tried to keep Jozef's presence a secret. But it was too late for that now. Jozef would never willingly give himself up, not after he had been chased through the woods by Johnnie Crawford. And if he was right about where Jozef had hidden himself, then he couldn't risk scaring him by bringing someone else along. It was too dangerous.

Charlie watched the water licking at the base of the rocks. It was time to go. No-one else could help. He had to do this on his own.

CHAPTER 10

The Pit

The faint hope that Jozef might have returned to the place he knew disappeared when Charlie made his way down into the hollow. The tin was still there and so were the twigs from the game he and Jozef had played. He could see piles of crushed leaves and the marks made by Laddie's claws, but there was no sign of Jozef. The abandoned space reminded him of the annual school play, when the stage was empty, waiting for the actors to appear.

Half-buried in the soggy leaves was the scrap of cardboard that had been hidden in the hem of Jozef's coat. He brushed the leaves aside and picked it up, staring thoughtfully at the incomprehensible words that Jozef clearly hated and feared, then he folded it carefully and stowed it away in his pocket. It was his only proof that Jozef really had been here.

Turning back the way he had come, he climbed slowly to the top and followed the faint trail left by their blundering progress on the day he and Jean had come searching for Laddie.

He stopped at the edge of the pit, staring down at the huge hole in the ground. Like most of the local mine workings, this must have started out as a bell pit, with people digging their way down, following the coal seam, digging more tunnels under the ground until, inevitably, the surface collapsed and the mine was abandoned. But coal was valuable. Eventually a new pit had been dug and once again the miners climbed down into the hollow to work at the coal seams until the day the pit turned into a death trap.

Charlie began to wish he had confided in Jean after all. He was taking a big risk. If something went wrong, he would be trapped with no chance of rescue. He would have felt much better if someone knew where he was.

There was no point in delaying things. He reached out and grabbed a thick tendril of ivy, giving it a couple of sharp tugs to make sure it was firmly fixed to the tree before he swung himself over the edge. It made him feel a bit like Tarzan, but this was no game. His heart stuttered in his chest when he felt the ivy begin to pull away from the trunk, but then it held firm, giving him enough time to anchor his feet on the roots embedded in the crumbling soil and take some of the pressure off his makeshift rope.

Sweat dripped down his forehead, but he couldn't spare a hand to wipe it away. Struggling to ignore his stinging eyes, he made sure his feet were secure before he shifted his grip and began to lower himself, using the ivy to support his body while his feet walked their way down the side.

There were plenty of roots to provide footholds. It was the ivy he didn't trust, but he forced himself on, inching his way down, expecting every second to feel his rope give way, leaving him to fall through space on to the rocks below.

It felt like forever before his boots finally reached solid ground. Staggering a little, he let go of the ivy and studied the tumbled heaps of rock that had been dragged out of the pit along with the coal. Charlie eyed them warily, wondering if they really were as solid as they appeared to be.

'Just as well Jean's not here,' he muttered to himself as he climbed up on to the rocks and crouched down on his hands and knees. 'She'd be galloping across.'

He moved forward across the first pile of rock in a cautious crawl until he came to the end, then slid slowly down to the ground, pausing to catch his breath before he began to climb again.

When he finally allowed himself to look back, he was encouraged by the discovery that he had made good progress. He couldn't see much beyond the rock in front of him, but he didn't think he had much further to go.

A short while later, he was crouched on the edge of a massive slab of rock, looking down on a riot of bramble bushes. He had no rope to help him now. Instead, he turned around and let himself fall, his body scraping against the rough stone until he landed in a patch of brambles with a jarring thump. He remained upright for a second, then his knees buckled and he toppled backwards into the bushes.

He lay where he was, waiting for his breathing to slow down. When he rolled over on to his hands and knees, he saw a sharp stone jutting up out of the bushes beside him. He had almost landed right on top of it. He shivered at the thought.

Pulling himself free of the brambles he climbed to his feet. Not far away was the shadowy hole that marked the entrance to the pit. The sagging timbers of the frame were splintered and riddled with insect holes. Stones and soil from the tunnel roof covered the floor. He walked forward and peered inside. There were marks in the dirt that might have been footprints, but in the fading light of the winter afternoon it was impossible to see clearly.

'Jozef!' His voice echoed down the tunnel. When the sound faded away, he strained his ears to listen, but there was only silence. Finally, with a deep sense of dread, he bent low and crept a little way into the darkness.

'Jozef,' he called again, this time in a hissing whisper. 'It's me, Charlie.'

He glanced back towards the circle of light that represented the outside world. If he went any further, he would soon be in total darkness. His brain was telling him he had to keep going but he could not seem to persuade his body to move forward.

At last his ears were rewarded with a faint scuffle somewhere not far ahead. He felt a surge of relief before his imagination took over. What if it wasn't Jozef, but something else? A picture formed in his head of the ghost of a dead miner, a walking skeleton dressed in rags, advancing towards him out of the darkness.

'Behave yourself, Charlie,' he whispered. 'It's probably only a rat.'

That thought didn't make him feel very much better. He half-turned, ready to scramble back out, but then he saw a pale face loom up out of the darkness.

'Jozef.' Charlie struggled to keep his voice calm and his body still. 'I've come to get you.'

What he really wanted to do was to grab hold of the other boy and drag him out of the pit, but he couldn't afford to make any sudden movements. He didn't want Jozef to run again. Not down here. Jozef coughed, a deep rattling sound that echoed round the small space they shared. He didn't move any closer.

'We didn't tell,' said Charlie softly. Even though he knew that Jozef couldn't understand him, it somehow seemed important to say it.

From somewhere close by came a pattering sound, the kind of noise that might be made by small creatures scurrying about. Charlie stiffened, realising that his imaginary rats might be real after all before he felt the dust settling on his head and he knew with an icy certainty that the noise was far more ominous than that.

'We have to get out of here,' he hissed. 'I think the ceiling's going to come down.'

Jozef must have been equally aware of the danger. He moved forward in a sudden rush, forcing Charlie into a hurried backwards crawl.

They emerged to find the sun low in the sky. Behind them, the earth gave a low groan as the ancient pit props settled even further into the earth. Shadows stretched across the ground from the entrance to the shaft, like dark fingers reaching out to pull them back inside.

Charlie stepped away from the hole and turned in a slow circle, looking up at the trees high above him, wondering how on earth he could possibly get back up again.

CHAPTER 11

Safe For Now

Charlie glanced uneasily at Jozef as he heard him let loose another cough. They couldn't afford to wait much longer. If they didn't get out soon, it would be too late. Nobody could make that climb in the dark.

He pointed back the way he had come and then up to the top, but Jozef set off in the opposite direction, threading his way through the maze of tumbled boulders with Charlie following behind, until they arrived at a place where the rocks lay piled one on top of the other like a series of giant steps leading all the way up. It was a tough climb, but nowhere near as dangerous as trusting themselves to an ivy creeper that could snap at any minute.

Charlie smiled in relief. 'Looks like we're getting out of here after all!'

Jozef smiled in return, then he bent down and tapped Charlie's boot. Making a cradle with his arms, he rocked them back and forth. Charlie realised that Jozef was asking if he had been born with his twisted foot. He swallowed the irritation he always felt when someone drew attention to it and nodded.

He watched Jozef mime pulling off the boot, then point towards the rocks. Raising his eyebrows, he waggled two fingers, like a pair of legs walking. His meaning was clear. If the boot wasn't there to protect an injury, then maybe it would be easier to climb barefoot. That might be true, but Charlie shook his head all the same. The boot was meant to straighten out his foot. He wasn't allowed to take it off, except at night. He didn't particularly want to anyway, even if it would make climbing easier. He hated it when people saw his twisted foot.

The route Jozef had chosen made it much easier to go up than it had been to get down, but all the same, progress was painfully slow. The damp November air and the lack of food had left Jozef weak and shaky. He had to stop every couple of minutes to rest. Charlie wasn't doing a great deal better. The boot felt like a brick attached to his foot. There was no way he could fit it into the tiny cracks that provided support for Jozef's feet. Instead he had to use his hands to haul himself up.

It wasn't long before his arms began to ache with the

effort, but he toiled on until, inevitably, he lost his grip and felt himself slipping backwards until his foot jammed into a hole and he came to an abrupt halt. He hung on, searching for handholds with his fingers, but when he was ready to move, he discovered that the boot was wedged inside the gap. It refused to come out, no matter how much he twisted and turned. He was stuck.

Jozef came scrambling back down to join him and watched Charlie bend to untie the lace. When he managed to drag his foot out of the boot, Jozef grabbed hold of it, twisting and tugging until he succeeded in pulling it free.

Charlie wiggled his toes, enjoying the feel of cool air against his skin. His foot was the same as anyone else's foot, except that his ankle was twisted sideways. When Jozef handed over the boot, Charlie took it in his hands, but he didn't put it back on.

'You were right,' he said. 'It'll be easier without it.'

With a sudden impulsive gesture, he pulled off the other boot, knotted the laces together, and swung them over his shoulder like the other children did when they were down on the shore. For the first time in his life, he was outdoors in his bare feet. It felt wonderful. He turned and grinned at Jozef before he set off again. With his feet bare, every little crevice provided support and he scrambled quickly to the top.

Jozef arrived beside him and Charlie heard the rattling in his chest as he struggled to get air into his lungs. When Jozef finally caught his breath, he made a sweeping gesture towards the tumbled boulders and patted Charlie on the back. Charlie smiled to himself as he bent to put his boots back on. He didn't know whether it meant "thank you" or "well done" but either one was fine with him.

They plodded through the woods, the shadows lengthening around them, until they arrived at a muddy little trickle that meandered between the trees. Charlie felt a stab of guilt when he saw Jozef kneel down to drink from it. Jean wasn't the only one who didn't think things through. He had brought nothing to eat, but he could at least have brought Jozef some clean water.

The shore wasn't far away. It was littered with discarded bits and pieces that people had no more use for. There might be something that he could find to carry water. It was probably better to go that way anyway. Nobody would be down there now that darkness was falling.

With a watchful glance up and down the road, Charlie stepped out of the shelter of the trees and set off for the other side. There seemed to be no-one about, but he had learned from experience that it didn't necessarily mean nobody was watching. Jozef looked equally nervous as he followed Charlie down the grassy slope to the beach.

The tide was out, leaving a vast expanse of dark sand and shingle. Jozef sat on a rock, watching Charlie wander around, poking among the seaweed and the shallow tide pools until he found what he was looking for—a discarded beer bottle, half-full of salty water.

Five minutes later they were back on the other side of the road and over the pit wall, hugging the shadows as they moved past the sorting shed, heading deeper into the sprawl of machinery and buildings.

When they came to a standpipe attached to the side of one of the sheds, Charlie stopped and forced the tap open. Water burst from the pipe in a noisy rush, then reduced to a trickle. Charlie rinsed out the bottle, filled it with fresh water and handed it to Jozef, who drank quickly, shifting anxiously from foot to foot, his eyes darting everywhere.

Once the bottle was empty, Charlie refilled it and moved on. Jozef stumbled along behind him, staring around in weary bewilderment. Charlie fought down a flicker of panic when he reached the first kiln and realised that the walls were too hot to touch. Struggling to remain calm, he hurried on and was relieved to discover that the door of the next one was open.

Charlie peered inside at the huge empty space, with

its blackened walls and soft, sandy floor. Jean had been absolutely right. It was clean and warm. Exactly what Jozef needed. With the door open, there was even some light and, more importantly, fresh air. The clank of the mine's winding gear signalled that the men were on their way up from the pit bottom. He pushed Jozef inside, handed him the bottle and put a warning finger to his lips.

'I'll be back tomorrow. Stay out of sight.'

Jozef sagged against the wall. Charlie leaned forward and put a hand on his shoulder.

'I'm sorry we got it wrong,' he said. 'I promise we'll get you to Edinburgh. I'll stay with you until we find David Levy. I won't let you down again.'

'David Levy...' Jozef's eyelids drooped. His voice was no more than a faint whisper.

Charlie left him to sleep. Jozef was warm and dry and out of the wintry weather. If he managed to get out of the pit without being seen, Jozef would be safe in the kiln for a while at least. Tomorrow, with a bit of luck, he and Jean would find something for him to eat. And that was more than enough for now.

CHAPTER 12

Bad News

Charlie arrived at school early the next morning, eager to tell Jean all about what had happened the day before, but there was no sign of her. He hung around the gates until he saw her hurrying towards him, dragging a crabbit-looking Maggie along behind her.

'I'm not well,' wailed Maggie as they drew closer. 'My tummy hurts!'

'Then you shouldn't have eaten that worm,' snapped Jean. 'You didn't have to do it, just because somebody dared you to.' She scowled at her sister. 'I bet it's still wriggling around inside you.'

Maggie's wails grew even louder, so Charlie contented himself with a brief thumbs-up. He was rewarded by a beaming smile from Jean. All morning she kept sneaking looks at him whenever Miss Moncreiff's back was turned. It was obvious she was desperate to find out more, but he didn't dare try to pass her a note. He shuddered at the thought of what might happen if Miss Moncreiff got hold of it and handed it over to Mr. Munro.

And that wasn't the only thing. The bent heads and the sound of ink nibs scratching letters in exercise books didn't fool him at all. He knew the whole classroom was watching them. After Jean's confrontation with Jimmy, they would be making up all kinds of stories about her and Charlie. He sighed heavily as he dipped his pen in the inkwell and began copying the handwriting exercise Miss Moncreiff had chalked up on the board. Life would be a great deal easier, he thought, if only Jean were a boy instead of a girl.

When the bell rang for the midday break, he found her waiting for him at the gate. There was no sign of her wee sister.

'Ma had to come and fetch Maggie,' she told Charlie. 'She was sick all over her desk.'

Any other time Charlie might have spared some sympathy for Maggie's disastrous experiment with the worm, but not today. He was simply grateful that it gave him a chance for a private talk with Jean.

'I found Jozef,' he said quickly. 'He was in the old mine. I took him to the kiln. He's hungry, but he's safe.'

His smile dwindled away to nothing when he saw

Jean's eyes widen in shock but there was no time to ask any questions before a crowd of chattering girls appeared, sweeping her up and away.

'I'll see you later,' she hissed over her shoulder. 'Same place as before.'

Thursday afternoon's arithmetic test was almost too much to cope with. Charlie found it impossible to concentrate. He couldn't stop thinking about that strange look on Jean's face when he told her about the kiln.

By the time he reached the shore, he had already fought off a mass of imaginary disasters. When Jean appeared, a lumpy sack dangling from one hand, he hurried towards her, questions bursting out of him almost before she was close enough to hear.

'Why were you upset when I told you about Jozef? What's wrong with the kiln? You said it would be safe!'

'It was safe.' Jean twisted the edge of the sack between her fingers. 'At least, I thought it was... but they've got a special order for more bricks. Da says they'll be firing up the kiln tomorrow afternoon.'

Charlie fought to keep hold of his temper. Why was it that whenever Jean got involved, something seemed to go wrong? He clenched his teeth to stop the angry words from spilling out.

'We'll have to find somewhere else, then.'

Jean took a deep breath. 'Charlie, I don't think there is anywhere else.'

Charlie didn't trust himself to speak. He turned and walked away.

His anger turned to dread when they slipped into the kiln and he saw the hunched shape huddled beside the wall. Jozef's face was flushed and his breathing hoarse. Charlie reached out gently and shook him awake. Jozef woke up instantly, a hunted look in his eyes. He managed a shaky smile when he saw who it was and turned his attention to the sack Jean held in her hands.

Its contents were disappointing: nothing but a hunk of stale bread and a few old carrots. Charlie's contribution was little better—two badly squashed slices of bread and jam that he had been carrying around in his pocket all afternoon.

While Jozef ate, Charlie lifted the empty water bottle and slipped quietly outside to refill it. By the time he got back, the food was gone. Jozef was crouched against the wall, watching Jean busy herself with a needle and thread, stitching the torn sleeve of his coat back in place.

She looked up at Charlie. 'I thought we should try to make him a bit more respectable.'

She finished with the sleeve and handed the coat to Jozef, then delved into the sack once more. This time, she produced a comb. Charlie watched Jozef do his best to drag it through his matted hair. Luckily, his hair was so filthy it plastered itself flat to his head, making the dirt at least a little less obvious.

Jozef gave the comb back to Jean and Charlie crouched down in front of him. He handed over the bottle, waited till Jozef drank, then pointed to the door.

Jozef nodded eagerly and Charlie thought it was going to be easy after all, but then Jozef reached for his coat. He pulled out the piece of paper and tapped it with a grimy finger, staring intently at Charlie.

The temptation was enormous. All Charlie had to do was nod and Jozef would follow him out of the kiln. Even if Jozef tried to run when he realised they weren't heading in the right direction, he didn't have the strength left in him to get very far.

It was the obvious solution—except for the promise Charlie had made the night before. Unable to make up his mind, he watched Jean reach out and take the paper.

'This is where he wants to go,' she said quietly. 'And he wants us to take him. Us. No-one else.'

Charlie didn't see how that was possible. 'We can't walk

all the way to Edinburgh.'

'We don't have to.' Jean grinned. 'Mr. Munro forgot to ask me for the change from the money Jozef gave me. We can take the tram!'

'Well then...' Charlie could hardly believe he was saying it. 'Looks like I'll have to skip school tomorrow.'

'Me too,' said Jean. 'I wonder what stories they'll make up about that!'

Charlie looked at her in surprise. 'You don't need to come.'

'Yes I do,' she said.

Charlie felt a familiar anger rising. He had seen her sideways glance at his foot before she bent to pick up the sack.

'You think I won't be able to manage because of my foot.'

Jean stood up. She didn't look away, or mumble the way most people did whenever his foot was mentioned and he saw with surprise that she was angry too.

'And you don't want me to come because I'm a girl!' Jean took a deep breath. 'But it doesn't matter what you think. You can't get to Edinburgh without me. Not if I don't give you the money.'

Defeated, Charlie glanced at Jozef and saw that he was on his feet, clearly expecting them to be on their way as soon as they settled whatever it was they were arguing about. Charlie did his best to explain that it was too late to go anywhere tonight. When Jozef finally understood, his eyes clouded in disappointment. He sank back down against the wall and closed his eyes, clutching the water bottle in one hand.

Charlie turned away. He was beginning to wish he had never made that promise.

CHAPTER 13

A Narrow Escape

'Where are *you* off to?' Charlie's mother glanced at the clock on the wall. 'It's not time for school yet.'

He stopped with one hand already on the front door and turned to face her. She looked at him intently, as though she would have liked to open up his head and see what was going on inside.

'This is an important year for you, Charlie. If you don't get a place at the grammar school, you'll be looking for a job when you're fourteen.'

'I know that.' She didn't have to mention that the only job around here for someone with a wobbly leg was working as a picker in the coal sheds.

'I don't want you to lose sight of what really matters.'

'Don't worry, Ma. I won't.'

It wasn't a lie. It definitely wasn't the truth either, but the problem was that he and his mother were talking about two different things. He knew the exams were important, but right now the thing that mattered more than anything was finding a safe place for Jozef.

His mother narrowed her eyes, unconvinced.

'I promised Donald Ritchie I'd help him with his homework. We're meeting up in the playground before school starts.'

It was funny how once you bent the truth, it got easier and easier to bend it even further.

'Well,' she said at last, 'The Ritchies are a nice family. You stick with Donald. He's a well-behaved boy. Not like some of the bairns around here.'

She sniffed disdainfully and turned away. Charlie knew she was talking about Jean, but this wasn't the time to defend her. He had far more important things to worry about.

He reached the main road and gave a quick glance behind to make sure no-one was following before he turned towards the mine. A chilly wind gusted towards him off Fa'side hill, bringing with it a fine, drizzly rain. The mild weather was over. For the first time, it felt like winter was around the corner.

The day shift workers had already gone down the mine, but there were still people going about the business of sorting and loading the coal. Charlie crept over the wall and darted as quickly as he could from one building to the next, checking around each corner before he risked moving on.

Jean was already at the kiln. She smiled when she saw Charlie appear in the doorway, then she turned back to Jozef. Holding up the scrap of paper, she began talking slowly and clearly, as though that might make a difference to someone who had no idea at all of what she was saying. Finally, she pointed to the door. Jozef nodded. He smoothed his hair, his eyes gleaming with anticipation.

'What did you do about Maggie?'

Jean smiled. 'I promised her a penny for sweeties as long as she managed to convince Ma she still wasn't feeling well and then I told Ma I was going in early to help Miss Moncreiff fill up the inkwells and put out the jotters.'

Charlie stood inside the doorway, keeping an eye out. The longer they stayed here, the more uncomfortable he felt. It was a great relief to see the tram appear in the distance, making its way slowly towards the terminus, where it would stop for a few minutes before returning to town.

'Jean,' he said, turning back to look inside. 'The tram's coming.'

'Don't worry. It won't leave till nine o' clock.' Jean pulled out a hankie, licked one corner and began to rub vigorously at Jozef's coat. 'We're going on the tram, Jozef,' she said. 'It's a bit like a train and a bit like a bus.'

Jozef snatched the hankie away. Charlie didn't blame him. Jean was behaving like a mother hen fussing over her chick. Jozef handed the hankie back to Jean and joined Charlie in the doorway.

'*Strassenbahn*,' he said, pointing towards the tram.

It confirmed what Charlie had already suspected. If Jozef could recognise a tram, then he was a city boy. All the same, that didn't mean that things were going to be easy.

Jean smiled. 'This is going to work out Charlie. I'm sure it will!'

Charlie sighed. 'It's not that simple, Jean. Edinburgh is a big place. Much bigger than the Haven.'

'Don't be so gloomy,' she said. 'Streets have signs, don't they? And we can always ask someone if we're stuck.'

Charlie glanced outside. The tram had stopped and the driver was leaning against it, bent over a newspaper. Then his view was abruptly cut off by a man-shaped shadow in the doorway. The figure stepped forward and Charlie froze in shock as he realised that once again he was face to face with the man who had thrown him out of the engine room on the day they found Jozef.

'You again!' The man grabbed Charlie's arm. 'I thought I

told you to keep away from here!'

Jozef shrank back while Charlie struggled to pull free. But the man only tightened his grip, squeezing so hard that tears of pain sprang to Charlie's eyes

'Leave him alone! You're hurting him!' Jean hurried towards them. 'We're not doing any harm.'

The man's eyes narrowed. 'I know you,' he said. 'Your dad's a brick maker. What do you think he's going to say when he hears about this? Trespassing is a crime. He'll be lucky if he keeps his job.' He glared at Charlie 'And so will yours.' He moved forward, reaching for Jean. 'You two had better come with me.'

He was too busy trying to grab Jean and keep hold of Charlie to notice the boy crouching beside the wall. Jozef jumped up and charged forward. He butted the man hard in the stomach, sending him staggering backwards. Charlie squirmed away as the man fixed his furious eyes on Jozef.

'Ye wee devil!' he roared. 'Just wait till I get hold of you!'

All three of them ran for the door. Charlie threw himself outside, closely followed by Jozef and then Jean. She turned and slammed the door shut.

'Help me,' she gasped, struggling to shift the heavy wooden bar that kept it locked in place.

'We can't leave him in there!' Charlie was horrified.

'Don't worry,' gasped Jean as she finally managed to slide the bar across. 'Folk pass by all the time. He'll soon be out. And anyway, the brick makers will be here any minute to load up the kiln.'

Charlie didn't want to imagine what sort of mood the man might be in when he finally forced his way out. From the sound of the heavy pounding on the other side of the door he was already in a raging temper.

'We need to get—' Charlie stopped, distracted by a familiar sound from the far side of the Haven.

'The bell,' he said. 'Jean, it's the school bell!'

'So what?' Jean looked at him as though he was crazy.

He pointed towards the tram. 'It's nine o'clock!'

Without another word, Jean grabbed Jozef by the sleeve, almost ripping it off again. The two of them sprinted towards the wall with Charlie following close behind. The tram was already on the move. In a last desperate burst of speed, they vaulted the wall and arrived on the pavement as it moved past them. Jozef leaped on to the platform, closely followed by Jean, who turned and reached for Charlie's outstretched hand. He made a clumsy jump, his boots skidding on the rain-soaked cobblestones, but Jean managed to grab hold of him and haul him up on to the platform before her hand slipped out of his and he collapsed at her feet in a sprawl of arms and legs.

CHAPTER 14

In the City

'Let's go upstairs,' said Jean as soon as Charlie scrambled to his feet and brushed himself down. 'I want to see *everything*!'

Relieved that they were now safely on board the tram, Charlie held back and let the others go first. He didn't like climbing stairs with people behind him. By the time he got to the top, Jean was sitting at the front of the tram, her head turning this way and that like a bird in a tree. Jozef was beside her, struggling to control the coughing fit brought on by their mad dash to catch the tram.

Charlie checked the road behind him before he joined the others. Nobody knew they were on the tram, but as soon as that man managed to get out of the kiln, people would discover that there had been three children, not two. They were bound to realise it wasn't simply a matter of skipping school. It wouldn't be hard to work out that Charlie and Jean's disappearance had something to do with the boy in

95

the woods. On top of that, they had been caught trespassing —in Charlie's case not once, but twice.

A memory popped into his head. Once, when he was very small, he had seen a woman standing outside with a baby in her arms and all her bits of furniture spread around her. It had seemed funny to Charlie, as if she meant to set up house right there on the washing green, but the people around her hadn't been laughing. Later his mother told him that the woman's husband had lost his job. The house they lived in belonged to the pit. Once the job went, then so did the house.

He moved up the tram and sat down heavily in his seat, his stomach churning, trying not to think about how much trouble they were in. He had been too young at the time to understand what being homeless and jobless meant for that woman and her family, but he understood now. A wave of panic rose up inside him and he jumped to his feet. He had to go back and try to sort things out. Whatever Jozef was running from, it couldn't be as important as his own family. After all, Jozef didn't even know that Charlie had made that promise to find David Levy.

But then Jozef turned round to look at him, a beaming smile lighting up his face. He flapped an arm at the world beyond the window. Charlie plastered a smile on his own face and sank back down. It was too late to undo what he had done. Even if Jozef didn't know about the promise, Charlie did. He was stuck; at least until they found the address on the piece of paper that Jean had tucked away in her pocket.

He kept his eyes fixed on Jean, wishing he was more like her. She never seemed to think about the past or the future. She was far too busy with the here and now. But when she twisted round to look at him and he saw the frown on her face, he realised that he was wrong. Jean was worried too.

'That man,' she said. 'Do you really think he can get my dad the sack?'

Charlie couldn't think of anything to say that might help. In the end, he shrugged.

Jean sighed. 'Well,' she said, echoing Charlie's thoughts. 'I suppose there's nothing we can do about it until we get home.'

She jumped to her feet, pointing out a patch of green behind a high wall. 'Look at that! They've got horses in there and I never knew.'

The clatter of footsteps on the stairs warned Charlie the conductress was coming and they would need to buy a ticket. 'Sit down,' he hissed, tugging hard at Jean's arm.

Jean did as she was told, digging her hand in her pocket

to make sure she had the money ready.

'Three tickets to Princes Street, please,' said Charlie when the conductress arrived beside him. At least he knew that much.

She studied them one after the other, her eyes lingering longest on Jozef. He looked back at her, his face stiff and guarded.

'Shouldn't you lot be in school?'

'We're taking my brother to the hospital.' Jean pointed at Charlie's foot. 'And we had to take our wee cousin as well,' she added, with a glance at Jozef. 'There's no-one in the house to take care of him. His Ma's not well.'

There was a long silence before the conductress finally made up her mind. She took the coins from Jean and handed over the tickets.

'Any nonsense and you're off,' she warned them.

The tram rattled onward. Fields and coastline gave way to houses and pavements. Gradually the tram filled up with people, but that didn't stop Jean's constant blethering about everything they passed; the shops, the tenement buildings, even the factories. Charlie squirmed in embarrassment when he realised the woman sitting next to him was listening in and so were most of the other passengers. They wouldn't forget the bairns on the tram—

and neither would the conductress.

At last he spotted what he had been looking for—a tall clock tower at the end of a tree-lined avenue. He tapped Jean on the shoulder.

'The next stop is Princes Street. That's where we get off.'

They stepped on to the pavement and Jean turned around, taking everything in. She gasped in surprise when she caught sight of the castle high above them, dominating the rocky summit of the hill that swept down towards a parkland dotted with trees.

'That's Princes Street Gardens,' Jean said. 'They're famous. My Ma told me about them.'

She took hold of the railings that separated the gardens from the street and peered inside, and then she turned round to look across the road. Directly across from them was an elegant building with stone columns and a set of wide marble steps.

'There's a picture house!' Jean turned to Charlie. 'I've never seen a film. Have you?'

Charlie didn't know if Jean was seriously suggesting a visit to the pictures, but he was saved from answering her when Jozef stepped into the road, almost directly in front of a car. The driver swerved and drove on, shooting an angry glance in their direction. Jozef stepped back his face white with shock, leaving Charlie wondering whether he had got it wrong. Maybe Jozef wasn't a city boy after all.

Jozef set off once more, leading them across the road towards a baker's shop, where he stopped and stared longingly at the window display.

Jean rummaged in her pocket and counted her money, carefully setting aside what they needed for the fares home. Jozef waited eagerly. In spite of Jean's efforts to clean him up, he still looked like a homeless tramp.

'I'll go in by myself,' she decided.

When she came out, Jozef almost snatched the paper bag out of her hands. He pulled out a sausage roll and sank his teeth eagerly into the warm crust.

Jean smiled, then she turned to Charlie and pointed out a woman in a fur coat, who was studying a dress display in the shop window next to the baker's.

'She seems nice, Charlie. Here.' She handed him the scrap of paper. 'Ask her if she knows the way.'

The woman glanced in their direction. Jean gave him a nudge. Unwillingly, he moved towards the woman. As he came closer, he saw her tighten her grip on her coat.

'Excuse me,' he began, but she ignored him and walked off, still clutching her coat.

Charlie wandered back to the others, suddenly horribly

aware of Jozef, in his dirty coat, with greasy crumbs all round his mouth. When he examined himself, he saw that his jacket was creased and covered in dust from the inside of the kiln. He hadn't realised how conspicuous they were until now. Apart from the state they were in, there were no other children in sight.

Jean either hadn't noticed or she didn't care. 'There's a man over there selling newspapers,' she said when Charlie walked back to join her. 'He's bound to know how to find the address.'

The two boys trailed along behind her as she approached the booth and smiled at the man. 'Can you help us please? We need to get to Acheson's Close.'

The man turned to serve a customer, folding the newspaper neatly and handing it over with the ease of many years of practice, then he turned back to the children. 'What you need is a street map.' He picked a tiny little book off a shelf and held it up. 'Only two shillings and sixpence to you.'

Jean smiled hopefully. 'I thought you could tell us how to get there.'

'Thought as much.' The newspaper seller replaced the book and turned away from them. 'Get out of here. You're scaring away the customers. Beat it!'

CHAPTER 15

Lost

Jean's eyes grew wide as they wandered on past one shop after another.

'I never knew there were places like this,' she said to Charlie, her eyes passing over a window filled with nothing but hats and handbags. She stopped to study a display of shop dummies.

'Would that outfit be something you wear in bed, or is it for a party? They look far too fancy for pyjamas.'

Jozef laughed out loud at the awestruck look on her face.

'Come *on*, Jean!'

Crimson with embarrassment, Charlie pulled her away. The way she was gawping made them even more conspicuous than they already were.

'People keep looking at us.' Jean had finally noticed the sidelong looks. 'I suppose it's because it's the middle of the day and we're not in school.'

But it was much more than that. The hem of Jean's hand-me-down coat had been lowered more than once and the sleeves were too short. Charlie's jacket was an obvious hand-me-down too—and then there was Jozef, with his filthy hair and his coat sleeve half-hanging off, still grubby from head to foot in spite of Jean's efforts to clean him up. The truth was, they were horribly conspicuous on this city street, with its expensive shops and well-dressed people.

In unspoken agreement, they began to walk faster. When they reached a side road, they turned and walked up, crossing the brow of a hill and down again, until they arrived at a street lined with tall, elegant buildings. There were no shops and very few people.

'Let's go this way,' said Jean. 'At least there's nobody else about.'

She set off, with Charlie and Jozef following behind. Charlie wasn't at all sure if this deserted street with its blind, staring windows was much of an improvement. Without other folk around, he felt even more exposed.

'There's another park over there.' Jean pointed across the road, where a set of iron railings ran all the way along the pavement. 'And the gate's open.' She turned to Charlie. 'They wouldn't leave it open if we weren't allowed in, would they?'

'I'm not sure we...'

But Charlie was talking to empty air. Jean was already halfway across the road. By the time the boys caught up, she was holding on to the railings, peering through the gaps in the winter-bare trees and bushes.

'Look over there! I can see a little pond—and seats!' She grinned at Charlie. 'We could do with a chance to catch our breath!'

Charlie nodded. It would be good to find a quiet place where they could work out what to do next. He thought about the newspaper man and his map. Perhaps they didn't need to buy one after all. He would have been too afraid to venture inside one of the huge shops on Princes Street, but maybe they could find a little shop around here somewhere. Going into a shop would be much easier than stopping passers-by and asking them to look at a scribbled address on a scrap of paper.

They slipped through the gate and set off down a twisting path towards the pond until they rounded a bend in the path and came face to face with a woman pushing a pram. A little girl dressed in a red velvet coat was holding on to the handle. The woman's clothes were dull: a tightly belted black raincoat and a navy hat pulled down over her ears.

Jean let loose a nervous giggle at the horrified expression

on the woman's face. The little girl frowned ferociously and then she stuck out her tongue.

'Cheeky wee besom!' Jean stuck her own out in reply.

'How dare you!' The woman's face grew dark with anger. She looked beyond them to the open gate. 'I don't know what you think you are doing, but these are *private* gardens. You have no right to be here. Get out at once, before I call the police.'

'*Polizei?*'

'Oh no,' groaned Jean.

Before she or Charlie could do anything to stop him, Jozef turned and ran full tilt towards the gate.

'Jozef! Wait!'

Jean took off after him, leaving Charlie to hurry along as best he could. By the time he made it through the gate, the street was empty. He crossed the road and headed back the way they had come. When he turned the corner, he saw that Jean had stopped halfway up the brae.

She was standing at the entrance to a narrow lane that Charlie had barely noticed on their way down. There was no pavement, only a cobbled road. Although the buildings on either side of the road were shabby and ill-cared for, all the doors were padlocked shut. A little way down, a huge lorry almost filled the lane. It stood with its tailgate down, half-full of furniture.

'He went this way,' said Jean, 'I don't think he could have gone out the other end before I got here. I would have seen him.'

That only left the lorry. Charlie guessed that he and Jean were thinking the same thing. It seemed to him that lately he had spent almost all of his time going into places he knew were forbidden. Telling himself that one more wouldn't make much difference, he walked forward and tiptoed up the ramp of the lorry. The pieces of furniture inside were all tied up, with broad cloth straps to hold them in place. He didn't see how Jozef could have hidden in here, not unless he had managed to scramble up to the top of the piled-up furniture.

'I hate Edinburgh.' Jean's voice behind him made him jump. 'Why are the folk here so horrible?'

Charlie shrugged. 'I think we've lost him.'

He struggled to ignore the voice whispering inside his head, telling him he had done his best to keep the promise he had made, that Jozef had left him, not the other way around and that now it was time to give up.

'If we can't find him, then I'm not sure there's anything more we can do,' he said to Jean. 'He could be anywhere.'

'But he doesn't have the address, Charlie. I've got it in my pocket.'

Charlie sighed. Without the address, Jozef had no hope of finding his way.

'Are you sure he didn't make it as far as the other end of the lane?'

Jean nodded. Charlie turned back to the inside of the lorry. 'Then he must be hiding somewhere in here. There's nowhere else.'

Together, they moved a little further up the ramp, looking for a corner Jozef might have managed to squeeze himself into, feeling along the ropes to see if any of them were loose. They were so absorbed in their search that the voice behind them came as a total shock.

'Don't tell me there's more of you.'

Chapter 16

...And Found

Charlie and Jean spun round. A small door had opened in the big wooden gates beside the lorry and a bearded face was peering out at them.

'If you're looking for your pal, he's in here.'

The man who stepped through the door was small, stocky, and very hairy; more like a bear than a human being.

'I found him trying to climb in the lorry. When I tried to grab him, he skited past me and through the door into the warehouse. Didn't take me long to track him down, though.'

'You didn't hurt him?' Jean asked anxiously.

'Well, he did put up quite a fight.' The man scratched his head. 'He might be a wee bit on the damaged side. But right now he's having a cup of tea. Not sure how safe that is, when it's Kurt's turn to make it.'

There was a low rumble deep in his chest. Charlie and Jean exchanged a startled glance before they realised the man was laughing.

He stuck out a hand. 'I'm Tam, by the way.'

'I'm Charlie—and this is Jean.' Charlie shook the man's hand, wondering what was coming next. At least he wasn't threatening to send for the police, like the woman with the pram.

Tam tilted his head and studied them, then he shrugged his shoulders. 'I suppose you'd better come in as well.'

Charlie exchanged a doubtful look with Jean before he stepped through the doorway. Once inside, he stopped in surprise. There was furniture everywhere. Wardrobes, dressing-tables, chairs and chests of drawers, all stacked one on top of the other. Some of the piles were so high they almost touched the ceiling.

'What is this place?' Jean whispered from behind Charlie.

'It's the auction rooms, lass,' Tam said in his deep rumbling voice. 'All this stuff has either been sold or it's about to be.'

He set off down a narrow passage between the stacks, twisting and turning through the maze. Charlie hurried to keep up with him. If they got left behind, he wasn't at all sure he would remember the way back out. Jean must have had the same thought. She was following so close behind him she was almost treading on his heels.

They reached an open space in the middle of the jumbled piles and there was Jozef, sitting quietly on a chair, steam rising from the cup he held in his hands. There was no sign of his earlier panic. He seemed perfectly happy.

'That's Kurt.' Their guide pointed to the man sitting next to Jozef. 'He used to be a merchant seaman before he met a lass from Leith and decided to settle down and raise a family.'

When Jozef saw Charlie and Jean, the flash of relief on his face was followed by a shamefaced grin. He turned and spoke to the man beside him.

Kurt listened carefully, then he said, 'Jozef is sorry he ran away.'

'You can talk to him?' Jean's eyes gleamed with excitement.

Tam pulled two more chairs from a teetering stack and then disappeared, mumbling something about cups. Charlie sat on one chair and Jean perched on the other, both of them conscious of Kurt watching them with a puzzled frown.

'How does Jozef come to be with you?'

It was obvious he hadn't been expecting two more children, especially children who might not be as ragged as Jozef, but were almost equally grubby.

'We brought him here—to Edinburgh,' said Charlie. 'We found him hiding in the woods near Morison's Haven.' If this man had worked on the boats he was bound to know where that was. 'There was no-one else with him when we found him. He was all on his own. We tried to get him to come home with us, but he wouldn't.'

Kurt nodded and turned back to Jozef. He kept his voice low and gentle, clearly choosing his words with care. Jozef listened, his eyes fixed on Charlie and Jean. When he began to speak, a flood of words spilled from his mouth, as though a dam had burst. Kurt did his best to keep up, listening carefully, changing what Jozef said into English and passing it on to Charlie and Jean.

'In Danzig there was a night of... violence. After that, his mother put him on a boat. The captain searched him, looking for money, then he threw him in the cargo hold. One of the sailors brought him water. There was no food, but he didn't care about that. It was a stormy crossing and he didn't want anything to eat.'

Kurt tapped Jozef's arm to stop him speaking. 'I think he was beaten, but Jozef has not said this.'

He nodded for Jozef to carry on and once more bent close to listen.

'When the boat docked, the captain told him to go.

Jozef hid in the woods. He didn't know what else to do. The captain warned him that if he was found, he would be taken to prison.'

'But that's not true, is it?' Charlie saw his own shock and dismay mirrored on Jean's face.

'There would be no question of prison,' Kurt said. 'Right now, there are many people being welcomed into this country, refugees like Jozef, who have lost their homes and sometimes their families. He would have been taken care of. I think the captain simply wanted to make sure that Jozef kept out of sight until the boat left the harbour and was safely on its way.'

'We think Jozef has people here,' Jean said eagerly. 'We have an address. Jozef brought it with him.'

Jozef began to talk again.

'He hoped he would find someone he could trust,' said Kurt. 'Someone who would take him where he needed to go. But there was no-one. Only you and your friend.'

Charlie found it hard to take in. Not so long ago, Jozef had a home and a family. Now he had nothing. He was lost and alone, with no-one to help him except two children who couldn't even speak his language.

'Why is he all on his own? Why did his mother let him go? Where's the rest of his family?'

This time, when Kurt spoke, Charlie saw Jozef's fingers tighten on the cup until his knuckles were white. Charlie wished he had thought a little more carefully before he asked those questions. He was grateful for the distraction when Tam emerged from a gap in the furniture with a china teacup in each hand. He handed one to Charlie and one to Jean, then he turned to Kurt.

'We need to make a move soon. Got to get those deliveries on the road.'

He disappeared once more and Charlie sipped gratefully at the hot, sweet tea. This time, when Jozef spoke, his voice was so quiet that Kurt had to lean in close to hear what he was saying.

'He says his mother is still in Danzig. His father is gone.'

'Gone?' Jean asked in surprise. 'Gone where?'

Kurt shrugged. 'Men came in the night. Men in uniform. Nazis, I think. His father tried to resist. Jozef says there was blood. Much blood.'

Jean shivered. 'But what about friends? Or neighbours? How could they let that happen?' Her eyes brimmed with tears. 'What kind of people are they?'

'They are people like you and me.' Kurt's voice was suddenly harsh. 'Some of them refuse to see what is happening. Some are afraid to interfere in case the same thing happens to them. But there are others. Those who believe in what the Gestapo do.'

The words floated around in Charlie's head. Nazis. Gestapo. The words were familiar from radio broadcasts about Germany and from whispered conversations he had half-overheard in the past few months, but he wasn't at all sure what they meant.

Jean leaned across to Charlie. 'I don't understand why his mother let him go. My Ma would never let anybody take me away.'

Kurt stood up and took the cup from Jozef's hands. 'The answer to that question is simple. There was only enough money for one.'

Chapter 17

Friends

Tam reappeared with a suddenness that made Charlie jump. He began to gather up the empty cups. 'We've got to get moving,' he said to Kurt. 'We've got deliveries to make.'

It was an order, not a request. Kurt turned and spoke to Jozef, his voice quick and urgent. Jozef replied with equal insistence.

'I told him there are people I can take him to,' said Kurt. 'People who can help him.'

Charlie held his breath, willing Jozef to agree, but it came as no surprise when Jozef spoke only a few words before he pressed his lips together, refusing to say any more.

'He will not listen. He says he will stay with his friends.'

The stab of disappointment was followed by a hot rush of shame. Jozef wasn't some kind of human parcel, something that had to be delivered before Charlie could get on with his own life. It wasn't like that at all. To Jozef, Charlie and Jean were people he knew and trusted. They were his friends. His only friends.

Jean must have felt the same way. Instead of trying to explain that they needed to get home as soon as possible, she delved into her pocket and pulled out the piece of paper, unfolding it carefully before she held it out for the men to read. It was bent and crumpled now, almost falling apart.

'Can you tell us where this is?'

The two men leaned forward and studied the paper carefully.

'Acheson's Close sounds like the old town,' said Tam. 'We do a lot of deliveries, but I don't think we've ever been there. Jozef says you caught a tram? You must have got off on Princes Street.'

Charlie nodded.

'Well, you want to head back that way. You've come in the wrong direction.'

For once, Charlie felt his previous visits to Edinburgh gave him something useful to offer. 'The old town's not all that big,' he said. 'The bus goes past it on the way to the hospital.'

'Passing through is one thing,' said Kurt. 'Walking there is different. I am not happy about this. Not happy at all.'

'Well we can't leave them here,' said Tam. 'We're heading

north. We won't be back till Sunday at the earliest.'

Once again, Kurt made an effort to persuade Jozef, but the boy only shook his head and kept his eyes fixed on the floor.

Charlie could tell that Tam was growing impatient. Kurt might think he knew Jozef better than they did because they spoke the same language, but Kurt didn't understand Jozef's terror of men in uniform. He also didn't know how much Jozef had come to depend on the two people who had helped him ever since he came off the boat. The need to get home was a constant, nagging feeling inside, like an aching tooth, but Charlie couldn't let Jozef down.

'We'll do what Jozef wants.'

There was a brief silence, then Tam said, 'You've done what you can, Kurt.' He turned to the children. 'Is there anything else we can help you with before we go?'

Jean opened her mouth and Charlie gave her a nervous look, wondering what was coming next. You could never tell with Jean.

But all she said was, 'I wouldn't mind going to the lavatory.'

'Of course.' Kurt turned to the others. 'Anyone else?'

In the end, all three of them took the opportunity for a visit to the toilet before Kurt led them outside. Tam was swinging the tailgate of the lorry into place. Kurt joined him, slamming home the bolts that held it secure. When they had finished, Kurt turned back to the trio.

'I still think you should go to the police,' he said. 'They are the best people to deal with Jozef.'

'I'm sure you're right,' Jean said. 'But Jozef doesn't trust anybody except us.'

Kurt hesitated, then he said, 'Wait here.'

He moved off towards the front of the lorry. Tam was already in the driver's seat, ready to set off. Kurt hurried back and thrust a scribbled note into Charlie's hand.

'This is my address,' he said. 'In case you need a place for Jozef to stay.' He looked hard at Charlie. 'Not all Germans are bad people, you know.'

The lorry moved off in a cloud of exhaust fumes. Jean turned to Charlie.

'I don't understand this. Jozef's just an ordinary boy. Even if his father did something wrong, why did his mother have to send him away?'

Jean was right. They knew now what had happened to Jozef, but they still didn't know why. Instead of answers, all they seemed to find were more questions.

Jozef pointed to the end of the lane and smiled hopefully. His blue eyes seemed even brighter now, with a feverish glitter that Charlie found deeply worrying. The cough that had tormented him all day still shook him every few minutes.

They set off back up and over the hill on to Princes Street, with Charlie struggling to ignore his frustration at the thought of all the time they had spent in the city, only to find themselves heading back to the place they had started from.

'The old town's up there.' Charlie pointed across the gardens towards the castle, wondering what Kurt had meant when he said it was a different place when you were walking there and not passing through it on the bus.

'We should have asked Kurt for the bus fare as well as the lavatory,' Jean said. 'But it seemed rude somehow. And it's too late now anyway.'

It had started to rain, a fine drizzle that seemed to find its way right through their clothing. Charlie shivered and plodded on, hunched into his jacket, until Jozef jogged him with his elbow and pointed at the figure of a bent old man wielding a brush and shovel. Charlie nodded. If anyone knew this city, it would be someone who spent their days walking its streets. From the look of him, he probably wouldn't mind how scruffy they were.

The road sweeper parked his broom and shoved his hat

back on his head. 'Acheson's Close? You don't want to go there.'

'Aye, we do,' said Jean.

'Well you don't want the new town. You want the old town. This is the new town.' A sweep of his arm took in the broad streets and elegant buildings. He pointed towards the castle on the hill. 'That's the old town up there. Acheson's is a wee courtyard, between the Royal Mile and the Canongate.'

The three children gazed across Princes Street Gardens at the jumble of ancient buildings straggling up the brow of the hill towards the castle.

'You can get a bus right over there.' The road sweeper nodded towards a bus stop.

Charlie and Jean exchanged a look. The old man sighed.

'If you haven't got the fare then your quickest way up is through the gardens. Cross the railway bridge and take the path all the way to the top. Then take the road down the hill, away from the castle. It's at the end of one of the wee lanes off the High Street, but I can't remember which one.'

Jean looked across at the gardens, then back at the road sweeper. 'Are we allowed in there?'

He smiled. 'It's a public garden, lassie. You should be safe enough as long as you don't pick the flowers—and there's not many of them at this time of year.'

'Thank you,' said Jean gratefully. She turned to Charlie. 'Let's go!'

'But you don't want to go up there,' the old man insisted. 'You don't want to go up there.'

The three children listened politely, but they were on their way as soon as he finished speaking. The road sweeper watched them cross the road and then, shaking his head, he turned back to his sweeping.

CHAPTER 18

Underworld

They stopped at the top of a steep cobbled path leading down to a grassy slope that dropped away even further, ending in a thick screen of bushes at the bottom.

The children hovered uncertainly on the pavement, watching a couple pass by. Curled together beneath a black umbrella, they walked through the gate and down the path with the total confidence of people who knew they had every right to be there.

'I can't see any railway line,' said Charlie, 'but the bridge must be down there somewhere.'

Jean stepped through the gate. She set off down the path with Jozef trailing along behind her. Charlie followed more slowly, struggling to keep his balance on the rain-slicked surface. By the time he reached the bushes, Jean and Jozef had disappeared through a gap, leaving him to catch up. He found them standing on a narrow iron bridge above a series of railway lines that separated one side of the gardens from the other.

'Hurry up!' Jean yelled. 'There's a train coming!'

Charlie heard a sound in the distance. It grew rapidly louder until it was battering against his ears like a thousand waves all hitting the harbour wall at once. A huge cloud of steam billowed up on either side of the bridge, transforming the human shapes in the middle into faint grey ghosts. Jozef let out a whoop of excitement and Jean swung herself around in a circle with her arms upraised, as though she expected the cloud to sweep her up and carry her away. The engine hurtled on, the noise faded into the distance and the steam slowly evaporated until finally it had disappeared altogether.

Jean stopped spinning. 'That was braw!'

Charlie grinned, realising how glad he was that she was here with him. Jean smiled back, then she turned and led the way off the bridge on to the start of the steep path that zig-zagged all the way up to the castle on the hill.

It was a challenging climb, even for someone with two good legs. There were steps at the first few turns to make things easier, but after that, the climb got a lot tougher. Every time Charlie checked, it seemed as though he had just as far to go as the last time. In the end, he stopped looking and concentrated on putting one foot in front of the other. It was easy to see why the castle was built all the way up here. Any raiders who managed to make it this far would have needed a good lie down before they were fit enough to start attacking anything.

He thought about the climb out of the pit and how much easier it had been without his heavy boot. But he couldn't do that here, not with the whole of Edinburgh watching.

Jozef was struggling even more than Charlie. Every few yards he had to stop to catch his breath. When they finally reached the top of the path, they found Jean sitting on a rock, waiting for them. She chewed on her pigtail, a worried frown creasing her forehead as she watched Jozef stumble towards her.

'Everything all right?'

Charlie shrugged. There was little point in talking about it, now that the climb was over. It was only when he saw the street beyond the gate that he realised he was wrong. They still hadn't reached the top of the hill.

'Come on, then.' He walked towards the gate that led out of the gardens. 'Let's get this over with.'

The rain had stopped, but the pavement was still slippery. Charlie took hold of the metal handrail set into the wall and hauled himself up. By the time he reached the top, his legs and arms were aching. He sank down on a low wall, waiting for Jozef and Jean to join him. Like Charlie, Jean was hot and sweaty, but Jozef was white-faced and gasping for breath as yet another spasm of coughing shook him from head to foot.

A chain had been slung across the open space leading up to the castle, with a sign hanging from it: "*Military zone. Strictly no admittance*". Beyond that, a narrow drawbridge guarded the entrance to the castle itself. He had expected something ancient and crumbling, but the walls were high and unbroken and the castle forecourt was bustling with soldiers in dark brown uniform.

He looked in the opposite direction, where narrow tenement buildings with tiny windows and overhanging upper floors towered above the narrow pavement. They reminded Charlie of a picture from a history book.

'That must be the High Street,' he said. 'The street sweeper said Acheson's Close is somewhere down there.'

A truck roared up the hill. Two guards with rifles slung over their shoulders emerged from a wooden hut and checked the driver's papers before they pulled the chain to one side to let him through. Instead of returning to the hut, they exchanged a brief conversation, then turned to look at the children.

Charlie felt Jozef stiffen beside him. Jean reached out to put her arm around him.

'Why are they looking at us like that?' she huffed. 'They can't honestly think we're going to cause any trouble.'

Charlie stood up. If the soldiers took even a single step towards them, he knew Jozef would run again.

'There's no point in talking about it,' he said. 'We might as well move on.'

It was still early in the afternoon, but in the shadow of the tenements, it felt as though night was already falling. A little way down the road, they came to a broad crossing where the new town pushed its way briefly into the old, before the tall, narrow buildings resumed their march down the hill, growing ever more ancient and decayed. Charlie looked up at the attic windows high above, wondering what it felt like to live all the way up there. It certainly wouldn't be easy for someone with a foot like his, but at least there would be some sunshine.

Every few yards, they came across a stone archway marking the entrance to a narrow covered lane. Each time Jean saw the rusting metal sign at the top of an arch, she hurried forward to take a closer look, but none of them seemed to lead to Acheson's Close.

'I wish we knew what side of the street it was on,' she said to Charlie. 'It's hard to see the signs from across the road. We might have to walk all the way back up to check them.'

Charlie glanced at Jozef. 'As long as we don't go near the castle,' he said. 'I don't think that would be a good idea.'

They walked on, past a fishmonger and a cobbler, then a butcher's shop hung with animal carcasses, the floor liberally sprinkled with sawdust to soak up the blood from the meat. In between were dingy wee shops selling piles of second-hand clothes, dusty books and broken pieces of furniture.

Further down, the second-hand shops grew more frequent. Their windows were filled with useless bits of rubbish that Charlie couldn't imagine anyone ever wanting to buy—rags and empty bottles, broken ornaments and tarnished cutlery. In one doorway, a grim-faced old woman dressed all in black sat in a tattered armchair, puffing on a pipe, like a dragon guarding its treasure.

Nobody suggested asking her for directions. It was obvious she wasn't the kind of person to give anything away for nothing. She watched them walk past and puffed even harder on her pipe, sending out a cloud of aromatic smoke that set Jozef coughing all over again.

Jozef stopped so quickly that Jean almost bumped into

him. He stood staring across the street and then darted into the road.

'Not again,' groaned Charlie.

But Jozef hadn't gone far. He was staring at a rusty, lopsided sign marking the entrance to yet another alley. When Charlie and Jean caught up, he grinned and pointed.

'Muir's Vennel,' Jean read aloud. 'Leading to Acheson's Close.' She exchanged a triumphant look with Charlie. 'Well spotted, Jozef!'

They peered down the steep, narrow turning, but the view was blocked by a heavy wooden door that hung lopsided from a single hinge. Beyond the door, the further reaches of the lane were filled with shadows. On either side, crumbling stone walls dripped moisture on to mossy cobbles. Jozef shifted impatiently from foot to foot, clearly anxious to move on.

'Well,' Charlie said doubtfully, 'It looks as though we're on the right track.'

Jean's face brightened. 'Not much further,' she said, 'and then we can go home.'

Charlie nodded. He, too, was more than ready to go home, though he felt his stomach knot at the thought of what might be waiting for them when they got there. He edged carefully past the door, trying not to breathe in the odour of damp and mildew drifting out of the stairway behind it. All around him he could smell poverty and decay, a combination of sour milk and rotting vegetables and the unmistakeable odour of too many people crowded into too small a space. Somewhere high above him, he heard a baby crying, but otherwise there was only silence.

Charlie was used to dirt. He had lived next door to a coal mine all his life. And he knew about being poor. Some of the bairns in the Haven had to take turns going to school because there weren't enough shoes to go round. But this was a kind of poverty he had never come across before.

His boots skidded on the greasy, broken cobbles and when he threw out a hand to steady himself it came away green with slime. He wiped it on his jacket and kept moving, telling himself that this gloomy alley couldn't go on for ever.

All three breathed more easily when they emerged at the other end. Across the street there was a huge stone building, its entranceway barred by heavy wooden gates. Rows of tiny windows overlooked the street, their glass covered by iron mesh. It was probably some kind of factory, or maybe a warehouse. Charlie couldn't see any houses. There was no sign that anyone lived here.

'Look!'

Jean pointed up in the air. High above them, an enormous

arch supported a bridge that reached from one side of the street to the other. There were doll-sized people up there, passing to and fro. He suppressed a shiver, gripped by the uncomfortable feeling that the street where they stood had been buried and forgotten long ago, while the real life of the city went on overhead, with no-one knowing or caring about the people below.

Jozef tilted his head, listening intently. From somewhere nearby came the sound of a shrill voice.

'There's a little sandy girl, sitting on a stone, crying, weeping, all the day alone...'

Charlie recognised the song as one that the children sang in the Haven. It was a comforting reminder of the world that still existed beyond this dark, unfriendly city.

Jean pointed to a gap between two buildings. 'It's coming from over there.'

They followed the song to its source, up yet another lane and into a square courtyard surrounded on all sides by tenement houses. The stone balconies running along each level were draped with washing; sheets worn so thin you could almost see through them and ragged underwear that Charlie's mother would have thought fit only for the rag man. Now that the rain had stopped, the washing hung limp and dripping in the damp air.

There was a girl sitting on a rickety chair beside one of the doorways in a small patch of sunlight that had somehow found its way through the clouds and down past the tall buildings to reach the ground.

Her face lit up at the sight of them. 'Hiya! I've never seen you lot before! Have you come to play with me? My name's Edith. What's yours?'

CHAPTER 19

Sandy Girl

It didn't seem as though this eager wisp of a girl meant to treat them with the contempt they had encountered elsewhere. Up close, her arms and legs were like brittle twigs and her head seemed too large for her skinny neck.

Jean must have thought the same. She smiled encouragingly. 'We're looking for Acheson's Close. Is this it?'

The girl smiled back. 'I've been sick,' she announced. 'I come out here every day. Ma says the sun will help me get better.' She stuck her bottom lip out like a three-year- old on the verge of a temper tantrum. 'It's boring here all by myself when everybody else is at school.'

Charlie wondered if maybe her illness had affected her brain, but then he saw her eyes sharpen with bright interest when they fell on his boot.

'Do you go to the hospital too? It's nice there, isn't it?'

Seeing her perched on that rickety chair, surrounded by these decaying buildings, it wasn't hard to understand why the hospital he hated so much would seem like heaven to her.

'It's all right, I suppose,' he said, moving closer. 'Can you help us find the place we're looking for?'

The girl waved vaguely. 'It's along there somewhere.' Her thin fingers closed round Charlie's wrist. 'But I don't want you to go. I want you to stay and talk to me.'

As gently as he could, Charlie unpeeled her fingers. 'We can't today,' he said. 'Maybe some other time.'

Her face hardened. 'But you have to stay,' she insisted. 'I want you to.' Her gaze travelled past him and he saw a gleam of triumph flicker in her eyes.

'Ma! Tell them they have to stay here with me!'

Charlie turned to see a woman walking towards them. She was dressed in workman's overalls with her hair tightly wrapped in a grubby blue cloth. She looked very tired— and very angry.

'Who are you?' she demanded. 'What are you doing here?'

'I told them to play with me, but they won't,' whined Edith.

Charlie had a sudden unwelcome vision of the three

of them trapped here all day until Edith went home and left them outside in the cold and the dark, unable to find the place they were searching for, lost among the bleak tenements of the old city.

Her mother quickly put that dark fantasy to rest. She scowled at her daughter. 'How many times have I told you not to talk to strangers? Where's your Grannie? She's supposed to be keeping an eye on you.'

Jean smiled at the woman. 'We wanted...'

She didn't get a chance to finish before the woman's face hardened.

'Looking for a bit of fun, were you?'

'No!' Jean protested, 'We only...'

'Only what?' The woman advanced towards her. 'Thought it might be a laugh to torment a poor wee soul who's desperate for company?'

A window slammed open somewhere above them. Voices began calling out to each other. Jozef didn't need to understand the words to know that things were about to get nasty. He turned and fled, with Charlie and Jean close behind. They didn't stop until they left the lane behind and were back on the street.

'I hate this place!'

Jean's voice was shaky. Her usual cheerful confidence was

fading away after one unpleasant encounter after another.

'They're not all like that,' said Charlie, trying to cheer her up a little. 'The men in the auction house were nice. And so was the road sweeper.'

All the same, she had a point. Perhaps it was something to do with living in a city, where strangers were more frequent, or the fact that they were on the street when they should have been in school. Maybe it was the way they were dressed. But whatever the reason, most of the people here, rich or poor, were definitely not friendly.

Jean turned away and began walking along the pavement with Jozef beside her, still struggling for breath, his face as expressionless as a lump of stone. It was as though there was no room left for anything except the need to keep going until they found the elusive address that had been sewn into his coat.

It was beginning to seem that they might never find it— and even if they did, they still didn't know what was waiting for them there. Charlie no longer had any faith in the happy ending he and Jean had imagined when they set out that morning from the Haven. With a sigh, he set off after the others. After all that walking, his leg was beginning to feel the strain.

Further along the road a wagon emerged from one of

the many turnings and lumbered on to the street, the driver tugging on the reins as it turned towards them. The wagon was pulled by a pair of matching grey horses like the ones that ploughed the fields in spring and autumn. Their legs were as thick as tree trunks and there were flashes of their huge hooves hidden beneath a dancing fringe of hair.

Instinctively, the three children crowded up on to the nearest doorstep to let it pass. Without any warning, the door flew open behind them. Jozef and Jean stepped quickly to one side, but Charlie fell backwards, landing heavily on a rough wooden floor. The stink of stale beer wafted around him and he caught an upside down glimpse of a smoke-filled room lined with scarred wooden benches.

'Get out and stay out!'

There were two men standing above him. One of them slammed his hand so hard into the other one's chest that he lost his balance, stumbled over Charlie and collapsed in the street in a boneless heap, half on and half off the pavement. Charlie barely had time to pull himself up and step back outside before the door thudded shut in his face.

The man in the gutter groaned. Ignoring the two boys, he gave Jean a gap-toothed grin and held out a grimy hand.

'Slipped in the muck,' he said. 'Gonnae give me a wee hand back up?'

Charlie didn't trust that smile. 'Leave him alone, Jean,' he said quickly. 'He's drunk.'

Jean hesitated, then she bent towards the man. 'Do you know where we can find Acheson's Close?'

''Course I do! It's the next one up. I can take you there.' The man wiped his hand across his mouth and held it out again. 'Come on, lass—I won't bite. Would you let a man lie in the dirt and not reach out to help him?'

Another wagon was rumbling towards them. Jean shrugged. 'I have to help him, Charlie. He might get hurt.'

Before Charlie could do anything to stop her, she reached for the man's outstretched hand. As soon as he had a hold of her, he was on his feet, his hands rifling through her pockets.

Charlie sprang forward, but it was no use. The man shook him off like a troublesome fly, sending him staggering into the wall. Jozef joined in, grabbing the arm that held Jean and sinking his teeth into the man's wrist.

'Get away fae me!' His face scarlet with rage, the man threw Jozef into the road, right in the path of the oncoming wagon.

The driver jumped up in his seat, hauling back on the reins, but the horses kept coming, unable to stop with the weight of the wagon pushing them from behind. Without hesitation, Charlie leaped forward and grabbed Jozef by the shoulders, struggling to drag him clear while his ears filled with the sound of rumbling wheels, heavy hooves and jingling harnesses, all blending together into one monstrous warning of what was to come.

CHAPTER 20

Dead End

Frozen with fear, Charlie watched the horses toss their heads, rolling their eyes as they struggled with the effort of holding back the loaded wagon and then, with a strength born of panic, he managed one last heave on Jozef's shoulders and dragged him out of the way. Together they crouched on the pavement, Charlie watching in horrified fascination as a massive hoof passed within a few inches of Jozef's head. The wagon mounted the opposite pavement, sparks flying from the wheel as the iron rim scraped along the wall, then it rumbled on, its driver roaring at them over his shoulder.

Charlie sat where he was, his mind blank and his body frozen, while the wagon disappeared into the shadows beneath the arch. Jozef lay beside him, ashen-faced and trembling. Jean was crouched against the wall. She drew a deep, sobbing breath. There was no sign of the man from the pub. He had melted away at the first hint of trouble.

'It's all right, Jean,' Charlie said in a shaky whisper. 'We're not hurt.'

Jean's eyes brimmed with tears. 'Oh, Charlie, I wish we had never come here.'

Jean was no longer the carefree girl he knew from the Haven. He remembered her gleeful smile as she hauled him up on to the platform of the tram, the gleam in her eye when she challenged the conductress with her made-up story of a visit to the hospital and the way she had eagerly soaked up everything there was to see when they first arrived on Princes Street. All of that was gone, sucked out of her by this harsh, uncaring city. Seeing her looking so small and defeated was almost more than he could bear. He felt the tears rise in his own eyes and reached up a hand to brush them away.

'Don't worry Jean,' he said. 'We're nearly there. Once we've got Jozef where he needs to go, we'll go straight home. I promise.'

Jean's face crumpled. 'You don't understand, Charlie. He took the money. There's nothing left. How are we going to get home without any money?'

Charlie had no answer to that. He sat in silence, watching Jean inch her way up the wall until she was leaning against it. Jozef struggled shakily to his feet. A trickle of blood ran down his leg from a cut on his knee, but otherwise he seemed to have escaped unharmed. He reached down and helped Charlie up, then he took a long look at Jean. It was clear from his determined expression that he was making up his mind about something. He took one step away from Charlie and Jean, then another, and waved his hand as though saying goodbye.

'He's telling us we can go.' Jean's voice quavered and she swallowed hard, fighting to get herself under control. 'But how can we do that? We can't leave him here on his own.'

She reached out towards Jozef, but he ignored her and began to walk away.

'Jean,' said Charlie. 'If that man was telling the truth, the place we're looking for is only round the corner. Jozef doesn't know that, but we do. And we'll get home somehow. I promise.'

Jean smiled a watery smile. 'You mean, even if I have to carry you all the way?'

Not so long ago, that comment would have made Charlie furious, but not any more. He was simply grateful to see Jean regain some of her spark. Reaching into her pocket, she produced a grubby hanky and wiped first her eyes and then her nose. After that, she linked arms with Charlie and together they set off after Jozef.

'Nearly there,' Charlie said when they caught up, even though he knew Jozef couldn't understand the words.

Jozef smiled at him, but Charlie couldn't smile back. Not because he was bruised and battered and the ache in his leg was now a constant pain, but because Jozef couldn't seem to stop shivering. It was as if he was freezing cold—and yet there were beads of sweat glistening on his forehead. Living in the Haven, Charlie recognised the signs of a fever. Jozef was sick. They had to get there soon, or it would be too late.

The next turning was a narrow gap between the buildings, not a lane but a steep staircase. The stone steps were worn down in the middle by the countless feet that had passed this way over the years, but when they peered up into the gloom, they saw nothing but a blank stone wall.

'That can't be right,' said Jean. 'Why would anyone build a stairway to nowhere?'

Charlie pushed away the worrying thought that the man from the pub might have been lying to them after all. He put one hand against the wall and began to climb, one step at a time. Jean and Jozef followed in silence.

He reached the top and was relieved to discover that the steps continued around the corner, up into yet another dingy courtyard. Charlie walked forward. The courtyard was so dark and dirty it was hard to tell where the walls ended and the shadows began.

He looked up and saw that the clouds had all disappeared, but the brightness in the sky made this little courtyard even gloomier. Jean was staring at the walls with a worried frown.

'There's nothing here. It must be a dead end after all.'

'No. Look...' Charlie pointed. 'There's something over there.'

It was a door, its dull green paint cracked and peeling. Beside it was a little window coated with dust and dirt. He walked across and pressed his nose against the glass. The sill inside was littered with cogs and springs. He could see two ancient clocks, their wooden cases so swollen with damp it seemed almost as though whatever was inside was trying to force its way out. There was no sign of any movement, but when he screwed up his eyes and peered inside, he thought he could see a faint light flickering somewhere at the back of the room.

He rejoined the others just as Jozef's legs folded under him and he sank down on to the ground. Jean knelt beside him and took hold of his hand. Once more Charlie saw tears glisten in her eyes.

'You wait here,' he said. 'I won't be long.'

He walked forward and gripped the handle of the

door. To his surprise, he felt it turn in his hand. His heart thumping in his chest, he pushed the door open and heard a bell jangle above his head as he stepped inside.

Chapter 21

Tick Tock

The noise of the doorbell faded away and the low-ceilinged room was filled with the sound of ticking clocks. They were everywhere—clocks with broken faces and dangling springs, all piled haphazardly on rickety tables. Others, much larger, almost twice as tall as Charlie, stood against the walls, leaning drunkenly into each other like a series of giant dominoes frozen before they fell.

One clock made a half-hearted attempt to strike the hour, its chime erratic and out of tune. From another came the sound of a single, heavy clunk. In spite of the non-stop ticking, not a single clock seemed able to agree with any of the others about what time it was. Charlie breathed in the smell of damp and mould and he shivered, partly from cold and partly from fear.

He reached up to brush a stray cobweb from his cheek and took a couple of steps forward, his boots clattering on what felt like a paved stone floor. The shop seemed to be empty, but there had to be somebody nearby—otherwise the door would surely have been locked. Wondering whether it might be better to go and wait outside, Charlie looked around nervously, half-expecting someone to pop out from some unseen location, demanding to know what he was doing there.

'It is bad enough that you children press your nose up against my windows and ring the bell all day till I am driven mad with your games. Now you are coming inside.'

The ghostly voice made him jump. There was still no-one in sight. He peered through the gloom at the tiny spot of light at the far end of the room, but the clocks took up so much space it was hard to work out exactly where the voice was coming from. As far as he could tell, its source was somewhere behind an ancient grandfather clock. Its ornate carving was splintered and chipped and the glass case at the top was so dirty the clock face was no longer visible.

Charlie walked forward, one slow step at a time, trying hard not to bump into anything. He rounded the corner and stopped in surprise at the sight of a cloaked figure hunched over a table. Above it a naked light bulb dangled on a wire. The shape raised its head and Charlie recoiled in horror when he saw nothing but empty sockets where the eyes should be.

'Well? Have you brought me a watch to mend?'

Charlie let loose a gasp of relief. No matter how awful this place might be, it was still part of the real world. This wasn't some monstrous nightmare creature after all. It was just a man, wrapped in a shawl, wearing a pair of black-rimmed glasses with heavy magnifying lenses.

Charlie gathered his courage. 'No,' he said, his voice wavering slightly. 'I haven't got a watch.'

The man put down the tools he held in his hands and peered at him from behind the glasses. 'What is it then? What do you want?'

His accent was unfamiliar, but Charlie understood him well enough. He swallowed and took a deep breath, but he couldn't seem to get any more words past the lump in his throat.

The man sighed. He picked up his tools and pulled his shawl a little more tightly round his shoulders.

'If you don't want anything, then please go and leave me in peace. I have work to do.'

Charlie's hopes for Jozef crumbled away to nothing in the face of this man's unfriendly attitude. To have come so far and struggled so hard, only to end up here in this dingy shop was almost too much to bear.

He could hardly bring himself to face Jean and Jozef with the news that this place could not be the warm and welcoming refuge they had hoped to find. But there was one thing he was sure of. Whatever came next, he would not leave Jozef to deal with it alone. He would not break the promise he had made. Jozef was his friend and friends did not abandon one another.

The man bent back to his work, his narrow fingers sorting through the bits and pieces in front of him. As Charlie turned away, his attention was caught by a thin line of golden light that appeared in the darkness. He watched the line grow steadily wider and realised there was a door in the wall behind the table. The door slowly opened to reveal a room that glowed with golden candle light. Charlie saw another table, this one laid with a clean white cloth. A heavenly aroma floated towards him. Someone was making soup. A little girl peeped round the door, her head no higher than the handle.

'Papa?'

The girl's eyes were the same electric blue as Jozef's. Charlie fumbled in his pocket. It was Jean who had the scrap of paper with the address on it, but Charlie had something else. Not trusting himself to speak, he pulled out the crumpled piece of cardboard he had found when he went looking for Jozef and dropped it on the table.

The man threw it a brief, dismissive glance and then he froze. A tiny spring fell from his fingers. He stared down, not even moving when his glasses tumbled from his nose and clattered on to the wood.

Charlie heard him take a deep breath. Long fingers reached out. Slowly, the man traced the red letter stamped on the card.

'*Juden*,' he whispered.

He unfolded himself from his stool and stood up, impossibly tall, looming threateningly over Charlie. 'Where did you get this?'

Charlie took a step backwards, alarmed by the burning intensity on the man's face. It took all his determination to drag his eyes away and move backwards until he saw two dim shapes hovering outside the window. He beckoned them inside. Once more he heard the jangle of the bell as Jean appeared in the doorway, with Jozef behind her.

Charlie saw her eyes travel around the room and then come to rest on him. She stood where she was, clearly reluctant to come any further.

'Jean! Don't go!'

Unwillingly, she began to move towards him. When she reached the grandfather clock, she stopped in surprise at the sight of the room beyond the shop.

'Over here,' said Charlie. 'Bring Jozef over here.'

Jean stepped to one side and Jozef moved out from her shadow.

'Papa!' The little girl's voice was insistent, but the man ignored her. All his attention was fixed on the boy who stood in front of him with his head bent, wheezing with every breath.

'Jozef?' The man's voice was soft, disbelieving. Charlie didn't think anyone except him could have heard it.

But Jozef did. He stumbled forward and the man hurried towards him, knocking over the table, sending cogs and wheels spinning everywhere in his rush to gather Jozef into his arms.

Chapter 22

Journey's End

One moment they were standing in the dark, gloomy shop and the next they were inside a room filled with warmth and light. A fire danced behind the bars of a big kitchen range like the one at home. Charlie rubbed his eyes, thinking that very soon now he would wake up and find himself back in the cold grey world outside.

The man carried Jozef over to a worn old sofa in one corner of the room and laid him down gently. A woman appeared from another room and stopped in surprise at the sight of the strangers who had entered her home. She was small and dumpy, with an apple-cheeked face that looked as though she would be more at home in a country farmhouse than a city tenement.

Her eyes shifted to the man, who was bending over Jozef, stroking his forehead, speaking softly but urgently. Seconds later, she was on her knees beside him. There was a brief, intense conversation in a language Charlie didn't understand and then she shooed the man away, flapping her hands at him, clearly urging him to hurry.

He rose to his feet and made his way quickly back into the shop. The wail of a fretful baby filled the room and the woman turned and spoke to the little girl, who moved from the doorway. She sat down beside a wooden cradle, rocking it gently back and forth, soothing the baby into silence while she watched Charlie and Jean with eager curiosity. Her mother stood up and disappeared into the back room. Seconds later she reappeared with a brightly patterned rug. She tucked the rug around Jozef, sat down beside him and took his hand in both of hers. Jozef was crying. The tears he had not shed in all the time he had spent with Charlie and Jean now flowed down his face.

'What should we do, Charlie?' Jean whispered in his ear.

The man was gone. The woman sat with Jozef, murmuring soft words as she wiped his tears away. The little girl rocked the baby, staring at them with her bright blue eyes, so much like Jozef's.

He turned to Jean. 'I think we should leave.'

The woman heard him. 'Stay,' she ordered, and pointed to two chairs on either side of the fire.

Obediently, they sat down. Charlie didn't know how

long they would be there, but he was grateful for the chance to take the weight off his legs. On the mantelpiece above the fire there was yet another clock, its bright brass pendulum swinging rhythmically from side to side. His eyelids grew heavy. He looked across at Jean. She smiled back, but there was a question in her eyes. He guessed that like him, she was wondering what was coming next.

It felt like a long time before the man from the shop returned, bringing another man with him. The woman let go of Jozef's hand and stood to one side. The new arrival placed a heavy doctor's bag on the floor and lifted the rug from Jozef's skinny body, taking in the scrapes, the dirt, the bumps and bruises.

'Where did this child come from, David?'

So the shopkeeper was David Levy. They had come to the right place after all.

'From Danzig.' Mr. Levy said. 'I have been hoping for news of him and his mother ever since we heard about *Kristallnacht*.'

It meant nothing to Charlie, but it clearly meant something to the doctor, whose face grew sombre.

'Surely now,' he said, 'the rest of the world must see what is happening.'

He reached into his bag and pulled out a stethoscope,

153

then he lifted Jozef's filthy shirt and listened to his chest.

When he had finished, he tucked the stethoscope back in his bag and snapped it shut. 'We need to get him to the hospital.'

'No!' Mr. Levy stepped forward. 'He will stay with his family now.' He swung round to face Charlie and Jean. 'I have visited the docks at Leith every day. There have been no boats from Danzig. I do not understand how he came to be here.'

'He didn't come from Leith,' said Charlie.

All eyes turned to him and he flushed, uncomfortable at being the focus of everyone's attention. 'He came from the Haven. He was hiding in the woods.'

Mr. Levy frowned. 'Where is this Haven?'

'It's down the coast,' said Jean. 'Near Prestonpans. We came on the tram, but someone stole our money and we haven't got anything left for the fare home.'

'You want money?'

Charlie's face flamed bright red. 'We don't want anything!'

He would rather crawl home on his hands and knees than take anything from this unfriendly, suspicious man. He stood up and made for the door. Jean walked over to join him.

'Let's go, Charlie,' she said quietly. 'We're not welcome here.'

'David!' The woman hurried over to the door and shut it firmly. She smiled at Charlie and Jean, then turned to her husband and let loose a torrent of words. Even without understanding what she was saying, it was clear to Charlie that David Levy was receiving a ferocious ticking off.

All the time she was talking, she was moving around the room, fetching bowls and filling them to the brim from the pot that bubbled on the range. She paused for breath and pulled out two chairs from the table in the middle of the room.

'Sit,' she said to the children. 'Please sit.'

David Levy sighed and pushed both hands through his hair. 'Alma is right,' he said. 'You must forgive me. We are deeply grateful that you brought Jozef here. It is a debt we cannot repay.' He held out a hand. 'I am David Levy, Jozef's uncle.'

Charlie shook it warily. 'I'm Charlie,' he said. 'This is Jean.'

David Levy gestured to the table. 'Please eat.'

Jean didn't need to be told twice. She sat down and lifted a spoon. 'Come on, Charlie. It smells braw!'

She was right. As the warmth spread through his body, Charlie felt himself relax for the first time that day.

David Levy disappeared into the back room. When he

reappeared he was holding a small leather purse. Charlie blinked. He had never seen a man with a purse before.

Jozef had been given something to drink and some medicine from the doctor's bag which had sent him to sleep.

'David,' the doctor said, 'can I have a word?'

The two men huddled together in a corner of the room. It was obvious from his Edinburgh accent that the doctor was a local man, but he seemed just as confident with that other language as David Levy and his wife.

Charlie watched them carefully. He saw Mr. Levy shake his head. There was some more discussion, then the eyes of both men turned to Charlie, focusing inevitably on the heavy boot on his left foot. He heard the sound of keys changing hands and Mr. Levy turned back to the table.

'Doctor Kaplan has very kindly agreed to lend me his car,' he said. 'I will drive you home to the Haven.'

'A car?' Jean's voice trembled with excitement. 'We've never been in a car before, have we Charlie?'

Doctor Kaplan smiled briefly at them before he turned his attention back to Mr. Levy. 'I wish you would reconsider taking Jozef to hospital. Your nephew needs nursing.'

Alma bent and stroked Jozef's face. 'He has me. I will care for him.' When she looked up at the doctor, her homely face was transformed by a dazzling smile.

Chapter 23

Homeward Bound

Instead of taking them down the steps, Jozef's uncle led them towards a covered passage that was tucked away, almost invisible, in one corner of the courtyard. Charlie saw Jean eye it doubtfully before she stepped inside. He didn't blame her. The passage was dank and deeply uninviting, more like a tunnel than a street.

He followed along behind her with gritted teeth, resigned to yet another long walk. It wasn't only that his leg ached. He could feel blisters rubbing on his heel every time he put his foot on the ground. But it could have been much worse. At least he wouldn't have to walk all the way home, not even as far as Princes Street to catch the tram.

They emerged on to the High Street to discover that they were only a short distance away from the lane they had followed in search of Acheson's Close. Charlie sagged in relief at the realisation that he didn't have to walk much further.

'All that way for nothing!' Jean said in disgust. 'We could have got there in a minute if we'd known about that other way.'

Charlie said nothing. All around him the shadows were lengthening. It was well into the afternoon and they had been away from the Haven for almost a whole day. His family would be frantic.

Jean's irritation had vanished as soon as she saw the small black car waiting beside the kerb. She watched eagerly while Mr. Levy opened the door, pushed the driver's seat forward and gestured for them to climb inside.

'Leather seats!' Jean grinned as she shifted over in the back to make room for Charlie.

He sat down beside her, struggling with his growing tension at the thought of what might be waiting for them at home. The man they had shut in the kiln would have reported them to the pit manager as soon as he got out. At school, Mr. Munro would be furious with them and so would Miss Moncreiff, not to mention Johnnie Crawford the bobby—and then there were his parents—his brother, his grandad.

Charlie saw a shadow cross Jean's face and realised that she was worried too. But her smile returned as soon as Mr. Levy climbed in and started the ignition. Jean was clearly determined that nothing was going to interfere with the pleasure of her very first car journey.

The engine coughed and the car jerked forward before it came to a sudden halt, sending both children sliding off the slippery seats.

'I am sorry.' Mr. Levy restarted the engine. 'It is a long time since I have driven a car.' He wrenched the steering wheel sideways, almost mounting the opposite pavement in his effort to get the car over to the other side of the road. 'And I am not used to driving in this country.'

Charlie and Jean exchanged an anxious look as they untangled themselves from each other. Mr. Levy kept going, driving very slowly, his knuckles white where they clutched the steering wheel. Charlie shifted uneasily as the car rattled its way down the ancient cobbles, wondering whether their anxious driver knew where he was going.

'Shouldn't we be heading back up the hill?' He kept his voice low, unwilling to disturb Mr. Levy's concentration.

'I expect he knows what he's doing.' Jean kept her eyes on the window, drinking in the view outside. 'It all looks so different, doesn't it, when you're in a car?'

She was right. The dark and threatening old town didn't seem scary at all, not now that he was warm and safe inside the car.

'What's that?' Jean pointed to a set of massive iron gates. Behind them loomed a vast building, a fairy-tale castle with turrets and towers and far more windows than Charlie could count.

'Holyrood Palace.' Mr. Levy said. 'That is where the King stays when he comes to Edinburgh.'

The beep of a horn behind them signalled that an impatient queue of traffic was building up and Mr. Levy began to drive a little faster. Charlie held his breath. He was too nervous about Mr. Levy's driving and too busy worrying about what was waiting for them at home to enjoy the journey. He began to calm down a little after they passed below a railway bridge and drove up yet another brae on to a wider road that he recognised from their tram ride that morning. It seemed that Mr. Levy did know where he was going after all.

'I must thank you again for bringing Jozef to us,' he said, relaxing his grip on the steering wheel now that the road was wide and straight.

'He was hiding in the woods near the harbour,' said Jean.

The man was watching them in the mirror. 'Alone?'

'There was no-one with him,' Charlie said, wishing Mr. Levy would keep his eyes on the road.

'And you are *absolutely* sure he was alone?'

Mr. Levy sounded angry again, but then Charlie realised that it wasn't anger. David Levy's eyes were filled with such desperate hope that he found it impossible to look away.

He didn't want to say it, but he had no choice. 'There was no-one else. Only Jozef.'

Mr. Levy turned his eyes back to the road. Jean glanced at Charlie, but he could think of nothing to say that might fill the silence.

'We skipped school this morning,' Jean was clearly making an effort to change the subject. 'We're probably going to be in a lot of trouble.'

'But why did you not tell anyone about Jozef?'

To Charlie's relief, Mr. Levy seemed to have got himself back under control.

'We wanted to,' he said, 'but Jozef was frightened of everyone. We tried to get him to come home with us, but he wouldn't budge. In the end, we decided that all we could do was wait until he realised he could trust us, but that was before things went... wrong.'

Charlie left it at that. The rest of the story was far too complicated to explain.

Jean sighed. 'We tried to keep him safe. But he was hungry. And we only had the money he brought with him'

In the mirror, they saw Mr. Levy's eyes widen. 'You tried

to buy food with German money?'

'Charlie told me not to,' said Jean. 'But I did it anyway. We got caught. Then our headmaster, Mr. Munro fetched the police...'

'I am not surprised.'

For the first time, Charlie heard a hint of humour in David Levy's voice. He shot Jean a grateful look, glad that she had managed to direct the conversation away from the disturbing question of exactly what had happened to the rest of Jozef's family.

Charlie could hardly believe it when he saw the wide sweep of the Firth of Forth and the outline of the pit winding gear in the distance. A journey which had taken them almost an entire day had shrunk to less than half an hour. He leaned forward.

'It's the next turning on the right.'

This was it. Charlie felt Jean stiffen beside him as Mr. Levy slowed the car and swung into the cobbled lane that led to the Haven.

CHAPTER 24

The End of the Road

'Charlie...' Jean's voice dropped to a horrified whisper as the car emerged from the lane and drew to a halt. There were people everywhere. Jean's mother was there, holding Maggie firmly by the hand while she dabbed at her eyes with a corner of her apron. His own mother stood nearby, her face grim.

The rest of the women—and all of the men—were gathered round Johnnie Crawford. His grandfather was standing with Charlie's dad, his bushy eyebrows drawn down into a ferocious frown as he bent forward to listen to what the policeman was saying. Jean's dad was there too. He must have left work as soon as he heard that Jean was missing.

The policeman was pointing first one way, then the other, the men nodding as they organised themselves into separate groups.

'I think we got here just in time,' said Jean. 'But I wish there weren't so many folk around...'

Her voice faded away as every eye turned towards the car. Mr. Levy took a deep breath, opened the door and stepped outside. Charlie and Jean climbed out to join him.

There was a stunned silence, then Constable Crawford marched across the washing green and clamped his hand round David Levy's elbow. Charlie blinked in surprise. He hadn't given a thought to how the people of the Haven might react if a stranger turned up with two missing children. It was going to get even worse when Mr. Levy opened his mouth and revealed himself to be a foreigner. David Levy had probably known that—and yet he had agreed to drive them home.

'Who are you?' Constable Crawford peered into the car. 'And where's the other one? The boy from the woods?'

'Jozef is with his family now.'

Johnnie Crawford's eyes narrowed.

'It's all right,' Jean said quickly, but she had no time to say more before her mother ran forward and wrapped her arms around her daughter, hugging her so tight that Jean could barely breathe, let alone speak.

'This is Mr. Levy. Mr. David Levy.' Charlie was rushing to get the words out before anything else happened. 'He lives in Edinburgh. The boy from the woods is his nephew, Jozef. The doctor let Mr. Levy borrow his car to drive us home.'

Charlie's grandfather appeared beside him. 'You gave us the fright of our lives, disappearing like that!'

And now it was Charlie's turn to be pulled into a fierce hug. When the old man let go, he found himself face to face with his mother. She looked him up and down and tried for a disapproving sniff, but she couldn't disguise the wobble in her voice.

'You'd better have a good explanation for this, my lad.'

Charlie stared up at her. 'I didn't have any choice, Ma.'

He felt his father's warm hand on his shoulder.

'I think maybe we need to thank this man for making sure Charlie and Jean got home safely, don't you, Mr. Crawford?'

Constable Crawford looked at Charlie's dad, then he loosened his grip on David Levy's arm.

'Thank you,' said Mr. Levy.

'You can take it easy, Johnnie,' said Charlie's grandfather. 'He's not planning on making a break for it. There's too many folk around.'

Johnnie Crawford unbuttoned the top pocket in his uniform and drew out a notebook, unsnapping the band that held the pages in place.

'I'll still need to take some details.'

Charlie needed to speak to his father. He was sick with apprehension. 'Are you going to get fired from your job?'

His father's face creased in a puzzled frown. 'Fired? Why?'

'Because of me,' said Charlie. 'Because we went into the brick kilns.'

His father threw back his head and laughed. 'Don't be daft, Charlie! If they handed someone their walking papers every time some lad trespassed on pit property, they'd have no workers left!'

A great wave of relief flooded through Charlie, washing away the guilt and fear he had carried with him all day. He smiled up at his father, who smiled back.

'Let's get you home, son.'

Charlie almost floated through the knot of people and out the other side. His brother Thomas was at the foot of the stairs, watching Charlie hobble towards him.

'Looks like you could do with some help.'

'I'm all right.' Charlie was determined to finish this journey by himself.

'Fair enough.'

Thomas contented himself with a brief pat on Charlie's back as he took hold of the rail, but he followed close behind him as he climbed the stairs, ready to catch his brother if he fell.

Charlie reached the landing and turned to see Johnnie Crawford busily scribbling in his notebook. Now that the excitement was over, people were moving away. Jean was still outside, her mother hugging her tightly. Maggie had drifted towards the car, her hand reaching out to stroke the soft leather seats. If Mr. Levy wasn't careful, he was going to have an unexpected passenger on the drive back.

The sound of the school bell drifted across the rooftops and Charlie realised with a shock that it was barely four o'clock. It felt like a hundred years since he had set out from home that morning.

Mr. Levy raised his hand in a farewell salute. Charlie waved back and then he staggered thankfully indoors.

Jean and Charlie sat together beside the kitchen fire. For once, Jean had a Saturday with no jobs to do and no little sister to look after. But she hadn't been set free to enjoy herself without a good talking to first.

'Ma said I'm turning into a wild gadabout.' She grinned. 'I don't even know what that means!' Her eyes flicked down to the heavy woollen sock on Charlie's foot. 'I know you don't like me asking, but how's your foot?'

Charlie didn't mind any more—not if it was Jean. 'It's not too bad,' he said. 'I've got a couple of huge blisters and my leg aches a bit, but I'll be fine for school on Monday.'

'I suppose everything will go back to normal now.' Jean was watching the fire, her face serious. 'Charlie, do you think bad things happen because folk deserve it?'

Charlie thought about the man who had caught them in the kiln. He had threatened to get Charlie's dad fired from his job. That man had helped to make a truly miserable day even worse, and yet all Charlie and Jean had been doing was to try and help someone else.

'No,' he said firmly. 'I don't.'

'Then why did all this happen to Jozef?'

Charlie couldn't answer that. Jozef had seen his father dragged off to an unknown fate. He had been parted from his mother, then beaten and starved and abandoned in a foreign country with nothing and nobody to help him. None of that was Jozef's fault.

'I wish we'd had a chance to say goodbye,' said Jean. 'We'll probably never see Jozef again, never know what happened to him.'

'Don't worry, Jean. He'll be all right. And I suppose we could always write a letter.' All the same, Charlie knew what she meant. It didn't feel right, not knowing how things had turned out.

'We did a good job in the end though,' Jean smiled at him. 'In spite of everything.'

Charlie nodded. 'We made a good team.'

Jean laughed. 'Charlie and Jean to the rescue!'

She reached into her pocket and pulled out a well-thumbed pack of cards held together with a rubber band. 'Want me to beat you at knockout whist?'

'Beat me? You couldn't beat an egg!'

Jean laughed again and began to shuffle the cards.

She wasn't the only visitor to arrive at Charlie's house that day. Later that afternoon, his mother answered a knock at the door and stepped back in surprise at the sight of Mr. Munro waiting on the doorstep.

'Mrs. MacNair.' The headmaster took off his hat and nodded to Charlie's mother. 'May I come in?'

His mother stepped back to allow the headmaster inside. Despite his dread, Charlie had to suppress a smile as he saw her eyes sweeping the room, knowing she was wishing she had been given more time to prepare for this visit. The smile disappeared completely when he found himself looking up into Mr. Munro's stern face.

'I have spoken on the telephone with Dr. Kaplan, who is caring for this boy, Jozef.' Mr. Munro looked down at Charlie, his face expressionless. 'I now believe you did the best you could in difficult circumstances. I felt I should let you know there will be no punishment for missing a day at school.'

'I'm glad to hear that, Mr. Munro.' Charlie's mother stepped forward. 'His education is very important to us.'

Parents were not encouraged to visit the school. All Charlie ever brought home was a written report. It came as no surprise to him that his mother was determined to take full advantage of a chance to speak to the headmaster.

Mr. Munro nodded. 'I understand that Mrs. MacNair. You can rest assured I will do all I can to provide Charlie with the opportunities he deserves.' He placed his hat back on his head and straightened the brim. 'Good day to you.'

And then he was gone, leaving Charlie and his mother staring at each other across the room.

'I hope you've learned something from all this. Life's not one big adventure, you know.'

'It wasn't much of an adventure,' said Charlie. 'Mostly, it was scary. But I didn't have any choice. Not after I promised Jozef I would help him.'

She gave him a nod. 'I'm proud of you, Charlie. You did the right thing.'

His stern-faced mother almost never smiled, but she did now. Charlie was so surprised he almost fell off his chair.

CHAPTER 25

Reunited

Jean was wrong. Life didn't go back to normal on Monday. The other boys couldn't take their eyes off Charlie, passing whispered comments to one another as they formed into a line and walked into the school. Charlie was sure that the same thing must be happening to Jean in the girls' playground.

The whispering carried on in the classroom until Miss Moncreiff finally lost her temper. She pulled open a drawer, reached for her belt and slammed it on the desk so hard that everyone jumped. For the rest of the morning she patrolled the classroom, eyeing the children, daring each one to be the next one to talk.

At playtime Charlie was amazed by the stories that were going round like a game of pass the parcel: he and Jean had run off together and been brought back by a police inspector in a big black car; they had been kidnapped by a gang of foreign spies lurking around the harbour and—most surprising of all—they had stumbled upon a ghost in the woods and been dragged off to an underground city where they had wandered, lost and alone, until they finally found their way back home.

From what Charlie could work out, the ghost theory seemed to have started with Maggie. When he caught up with Jean on the way home, he wasn't surprised to discover that the idea had come from her big sister.

'Well, I thought if they were going to be making up stories, I might as well join in and make up some good ones,' she told him.

'Seems like I'm not the only one with too much imagination,' he said with a grin.

November gave way to December. Life seemed to have settled down once more, until the day Charlie stood leaning against the playground wall, trying to decide whether he should keep standing, or sit down to read his book and try to ignore the biting wind.

Without any warning, the book was knocked from his hands. He looked up to see Jimmy Doig standing in front of him. All around him, loose pages from his precious book were fluttering across the playground.

Charlie's face flushed with anger. 'You think you're a big man, do you, Jimmy?'

He knew there was no way he could ever fight Jimmy and win. But even though he wasn't as strong as Jimmy, that didn't mean he was going to let him get away with it. He knew he was going to get thumped and he knew it was going to hurt. But he also knew that it would be worth it.

'Mud sticks,' he said to Jimmy. 'Everybody knows you're a coward.'

'What was that?' Jimmy's face twisted into a frown, puzzled by the fact that his victim wasn't shrinking away from him. He moved closer. Around them, the other boys watched in silence.

'Do you think it makes you tough, Jimmy?' Charlie asked. 'Knocking down a cripple? Why is it that you only ever pick on people you know you can beat?'

Charlie braced himself as Jimmy's eyes blazed. He punched Charlie hard in the chest, sending him crashing back against the wall. His back thumped into the stone and he fell sideways, scraping his cheek on the wall as he went down. Around him he heard murmurs of disapproval from the watching crowd.

Jimmy stepped closer. 'You think you're a big man, don't you? Well you're not—you're just a great big Jessie, hanging around with the lassies because none of the lads want to have anything to do with you.'

'Jean's a friend of mine,' said Charlie. 'But you wouldn't know about that, would you Jimmy? Because you don't have any friends.'

Jimmy scanned the circle of boys, as though he expected them to urge him on. Nobody did. He scowled.

'Anyone else want some?' He raised his clenched fists.

When no-one answered, he aimed another half-hearted kick at Charlie and walked away.

Someone grabbed hold of Charlie's jacket and hauled him to his feet.

'Don't worry about Jimmy,' said Donald Ritchie. 'He's jealous.'

'Jealous?' Charlie didn't know what he had expected, but it wasn't that.

Donald laughed. 'You fought a ghost in the woods and survived!'

For what felt like the hundredth time, Charlie said, 'there wasn't any ghost. We found a boy in the woods. He was lost, so we took him to his uncle in Edinburgh.'

One of the other boys handed him the torn pages from his book. 'It was an enemy agent, not a ghost!' he said firmly.

Charlie knew he might as well save his breath. Nobody

wanted to hear what really happened. The stories people were passing on were so much better than the truth.

'Charlie MacNair!' Miss Moncreiff's shrill voice rose above the playground noise. 'Mr. Munro wants to see you.'

Charlie bumped into Jean in the corridor. She looked him up and down, taking in his rumpled clothes and the raw and bleeding graze on his cheek.

'What happened to you?'

'Just sorting something out,' he said with a smile, then he grimaced and put his hand up to his face. It was going to be sore for days. All the same, Jimmy Doig would think twice before he went to hit Charlie again.

'You'd better clean yourself up before Mr. Munro sees you.'

Charlie straightened his jacket and flattened his hair as they walked together down the corridor. He couldn't help feeling a little anxious when he remembered the last time he had been called to the headmaster's office.

Mr. Munro was at his desk and Charlie was very glad to see that this time there was no sign of the belt. The headmaster lifted his eyebrows when he saw the scrape on Charlie's face, but all he said was, 'I have some visitors here who would like to speak to you.'

There were two other people in the room. A tall, man

dressed in a worn-out black suit that was shiny with age, and a boy. The man was David Levy. The boy was Jozef. His clothes were clean and neat, his hair brushed and his shoes shining, but Jean and Charlie would have known him anywhere.

'Hello Charlie. Hello Jean.' Jozef's tongue stumbled over the unfamiliar words. 'Thank you for being my friends.'

Jean ran forward and wrapped her arms around him before she remembered where she was. She looked at Mr. Munro nervously, but he was smiling too, a stiff little smile, as though he didn't get much practice.

Charlie stepped forward, grinning so widely he felt sure everyone could see right to the back of his throat. He held out a hand. Jozef reached out and shook it vigorously.

'Jozef has told us all about how hard you struggled to help him,' said David Levy.

'Have you found his mother yet?'

A shadow darkened Mr. Levy's face. 'We have heard nothing about the whereabouts of Jozef's mother Rachel.'

'Why did the police take his father away? What had he done?'

The man's eyes widened. 'You do not know that we are Jews?'

Charlie blinked in surprise. He had never heard of Jews,

except in bible class. He knew Jesus was born a Jew, but that was long ago. He had never thought that they were people living in the modern world, going about their daily business like everyone else. And it still didn't feel like an explanation. He didn't understand why being a Jew would be a problem.

'But that's only...' Charlie fumbled for the right words, '...a different religion, isn't it?'

'To you or to me, maybe.' Mr. Levy said. 'Not to others. There are Jews in hiding all over Europe.' His voice grew hoarse as he struggled to control his emotions. 'I hope my sister Rachel is one of them.'

'There are many Jewish children coming into Britain for safety,' said Mr. Munro. 'The government has agreed to find homes for them.'

'But what about their parents?' Jean demanded. 'Why don't they come too?'

Mr. Munro hesitated, as though he wasn't sure what to tell them. At last he said, 'They were not allowed to come with the children.'

The silence that followed was broken by the scrape of the headmaster's chair as he rose to his feet. 'Well,' he said. 'It seems that Jozef was anxious to thank his friends for looking after him. So here he is.'

Jean turned to Mr. Levy. 'We will see Jozef again, won't we?'

'I am sure you will.' David Levy smiled down at her. 'You will always be welcome in our home. You have brought us a brand from the burning.'

Mr. Munro saw the puzzled look that passed between Charlie and Jean.

'Mr. Levy is quoting from the bible,' he said, directing an enquiring glance at David Levy. 'The Book of Amos, I believe.'

Mr. Levy nodded and Mr. Munro turned his eyes back to Charlie and Jean. He paused before he spoke again.

'He means that Jozef has been rescued from a catastrophe that is unfolding all across Europe.'

Charlie thought of that damp and grubby courtyard with the gloomy little shop, of how different everything had become when they stepped into the golden light of the inner room. Jozef was safe now, whatever was happening elsewhere.

'We'll see you soon, Jozef,' he said, knowing that his friend might not understand the words, but would understand his smile.

Jozef smiled back. The school bell signalled the end of playtime. Outside the window, the playground grew quiet.

Jean and Charlie made their way back to the classroom,

talking quietly so as not to disturb the heavy silence in the corridor.

Jean stopped with one hand on the door to the classroom. 'What do you think Mr. Levy meant, Charlie? About a catastrophe in Europe?'

'I'm not sure, Jean.' Charlie's mind flashed back to the day they had found Jozef, the day he had seen the warships making their way to the open sea. 'But I have a feeling we're going to find out soon enough.'

The End

Author's Note

To many people, *Kristallnacht*, the 'Night of Broken Glass' was the night the Holocaust truly began.

In 1938, Herschel Grynszpan, a 17-year-old Polish Jew, shot a German diplomat in Paris in a protest against the treatment of his family by the Nazi government. This act triggered a wave of violence towards Jews. Orchestrated by the German government, the violence spread across Germany and beyond, and in the years that followed, more than 6 million European Jews were murdered.

The name on my birth certificate is Anne-Marie Grynszpan. Yad Vashem, the World Holocaust Remembrance Center (http://www.yadvashem.org/) lists my grandfather as Hershel Grynszpan's uncle. I do not know if this is true, but some family members believe that it is.

Acknowledgements

I am deeply grateful to Helen MacKinven and Anne Glennie of Cranachan Publishing, not just for the skill and sensitivity of their work on the layout and editing of *Charlie's Promise* but also for their huge enthusiasm for the story.

I would also like to mention my husband, who was my first reader, and Alex Nye, for her generous cover quote.

Thanks, guys!

About the Author

Annemarie Allan's first novel, *Hox*, was the winner of the Kelpies Prize in 2007. She writes for both children and adults, taking her inspiration from the landscape and culture of Scotland, both past and present. *Charlie's Promise* is her fourth novel.

You can find out more about Annemarie and her writing at:

@aldhammer
www.facebook.com/annemarie.allan.56
www.annemarieallan.com

yesteryear

Also available in the Yesteryear Series

Fir for Luck
by Barbara Henderson

The heart-wrenching tale of a girl's courage to save her village from the Highland Clearances.

The Revenge of Tirpitz
by M. L. Sloan

The thrilling WW2 story of a boy's role in the sinking of the warship Tirpitz.

The Beast on the Broch
by John K. Fulton

Scotland, 799 AD. Talorca befriends a strange Pictish beast; together, they fight off Viking raiders.

Thank You for Reading

As we say at Cranachan,
'the proof of the pudding is in the reading'
and we hope that you enjoyed *Charlie's Promise.*

Please tell all your friends and tweet us with your
#charliespromise feedback, or better still, write an online
review to help spread the word!

We only publish books which excite and inspire us, so
if you'd like to experience other unique and
thought-provoking books, please visit our website:

cranachanpublishing.co.uk

and follow us
@cranachanbooks
for news of our forthcoming titles.

cranachan